The team of Riordan and Masuda, both closet musicians, investigates a rumor that there will be some sort of nasty business during the annual Carmel Bach Festival. Many truly suspicious characters are discovered, along with several dead bodies. Our hero and heroine emerge victorious once again, however. So, what were you expecting?

Stab
in the
Bach

Other books by Roy Gilligan:

Chinese Restaurants Never Serve Breakfast
Live Oaks Also Die
Poets Never Kill
Happiness is Often Deadly
Playing God . . . and Other Games
Just Another Murder in Miami
Dead Heat from Big Sur

Roy Gilligan

Stab
in the
Bach

Brendan Books
San Jose, CA

Art direction by Robin Gilligan
Cover art by Reed Farrington
Photography by Splash Studios
Book design and typography by Jim Cook/Santa Barbara

Manufactured in the United States of America.

1-96

Library of Congress Catalog Card Number: 96-085135
ISBN 0-9626136-6-5

This book is dedicated to all the friends of the years that are piling up on me. Some of them aren't around anymore. And, lest I forget, I must extend this dedication to all the folks who bought this book. May your camels outrace a Triple Crown winner, if there ever is one again.

AUTHOR'S NOTE

Many readers will discover soon into this book that two of the characters are named after the unforgettable leads in Mel Brooks's first film, *The Producers*. Other rather more literary references are self-explanatory. The Bach Festival is an actual event, but there are usually no murders involved.

It is with deep gratitude that I bow to the illustrious Reed Farrington for his cover painting. I am amazed at how he managed to conceal the nude behind the cello. My love to my creative daughter, Robin, for the cover stuff. A tip of the hat to Will Smith, who has heretofore edited this series. Time crept up on the author so that he had to depend on the device on his computer. Any errors detected are the responsibility of Apple, Cupertino, California. And, of course, a low bow to Cheryl Masuda Yemoto, who is a lot like Reiko.

Stab
in the
𝕭𝖆𝖈𝖍

1

"I need my space, Pat."

WHEN I opened the office door, Reiko was standing behind her desk, telephone pressed to her right ear, left palm pressed over left ear with fingers of left hand pointing in all directions.

"I don't know what to tell you, Lance." Pause. "Well, dammit, I cannot help you. You're the judge!" Pause. "No, I didn't watch it on TV. It was all a bunch of bullshit, anyhow. I've got better things to do with my time." Pause. "Like makin' a living. Like workin'." Pause. "Lance, It doesn't make a damn bit of difference what I think. You can't tell a jury how to vote." Pause. "Family or not, I can't do anything for you." She was close to shouting now. "I hate L.A.! You have to live there. Give my love to everybody."

When Reiko saw me she uncovered her left ear and gave me a small wave. I approached and put my hand on her shoulder. She kissed me lightly on the cheek and made an awful face. I tried to sit on that abominable stool she uses at her desk and nearly went over backwards.

"Wait a minute, Lance," she said. Clamping her left hand firmly over the mouthpiece of the phone, she hissed at me. "It's my cousin. He has always depended on me to sympathize after he's had a rough time. I did it when we were kids, and he expects me to do it now. He's tired, Pat. That long damn trial took a lot out of him. God, it's been over for months! Now shut up."

Reiko clapped the receiver to her ear again. "I'm back, cuz." During the next forty or fifty seconds she sighed heavily and rolled her eyes as she listened to her relative pour out his misery. Finally: "I understand, pal. Just kick back and say t'hell with it. Get it out of your mind. It's over. Over! Got it?" Pause. "Yeah, you too. Bye."

She pushed me off her stool and sat down, drawing the back of her hand across her forehead to suggest exhaustion. "The poor sonofabitch," she said, "He tried the murder case of the century and now he thinks he's got an ulcer."

I thought about last summer. Somehow it was busier than usual. We had more divorce cases than we could handle. People all over the Monterey Peninsula were getting divorces, or trying to find grounds for divorce where one party was reluctant. It's not uncommon in families where a lot of money is involved. No "amicable" stuff, no "mutual agreement" or any such slop. In most cases one spouse or the other wants the lion's share of the community property. Somebody told me once that the "lion's share" really meant all of whatever people were fighting about. I guess that's right. But for Riordan and Masuda (or Masuda and Riordan), it paid the rent, with a little left over.

Reiko disentangled herself from the phone cord and gave me a hug.

"Missed you yesterday, shamus. Where'd you go? I left a message on your machine."

"Look, kid, if you'd move in with me, there'd be no problem. I've got your Japanese garden. I've got a house that's bigger than I really need. You're welcome. But you insist on staying in that upstairs apartment in Pacific Grove. Some day I won't be able to climb those stairs, sweetie. Then you'll be sorry."

I am perhaps super-conscious of the difference in our ages. I'm not exactly senile, but I am in—what's the euphemism?— late middle age.

"I need my space, Pat. You know how I feel about you, but I guess I'm sort of like Sally Morse. I like to be with you, but I'm not sure I can live with you. I've lived alone for a lot of years. Give me a little time. Who knows?" Sally moved to Los Angeles last year. Served her right.

I shrugged and went into my one-third of the office. Yeah, Reiko and I are equal partners, but she's more equal than I am.

The reason Reiko couldn't find me on the previous evening is that I was having dinner with Roger Carrington, one of my oldest friends on the Peninsula. Roger is the Exalted Commander of the White Knights, an informal group committed to various forms of mischief in Carmel, California, where I live. He is also a classical music buff and active in the organization and promotion of the Carmel Bach Festival, an annual midsummer event that draws aficionados from many parts of the globe.

I was surprised when Roger called me. He and I are not what you might call social. We respect each other and dearly love long conversations at Cardinale's on a sunny afternoon. But he had never asked me to dinner before, and when he called he was pretty evasive about what was on his mind.

When I met him in the bar at Simpson's, Roger did not seem to be his ordinarily jocular self. His manner was subdued, almost furtive. Other than a monosyllabic greeting he said nothing as we were led to a table. I began to feel uneasy, as though something just a wee bit sinister was about to happen.

We sat at a corner table, well away from other restaurant patrons. Roger knows I don't drink, so we skipped that ceremony, although I could see the old boy was dying for a martini. We ordered . . . I forget what. I really do. I was so caught up in the air of mystery that Roger seemed to communicate that I wasn't very hungry.

Finally, he spoke: "Patrick, I see you have some questions about my inviting you to dinner." He smiled weakly. "I thought you could use a free meal." The smile faded. Roger took a deep breath. "You know I'm interested in the Bach Festival. I love the music, Pat. I've lived here for twelve years, but I had a vacation cottage here for thirty years before that. I've been to a lot of Bach Festivals."

Carrington seemed to drift away for a moment. It was as if he were listening to faraway music. His eyes were focussed somewhere in the middle distance, perhaps contemplating the fairy-tale mural on the wall behind me. He sighed.

"Patrick, I'm worried. I can't tell you where I got the information. I can't even tell you why I believe what I'm about to tell you. But there is likely to be trouble at this year's Festival. Big trouble. A murder. Or a bomb."

There was a lengthy silence. Roger had said what ˌhe had come to say, and I couldn't think of anything to say.

"You wouldn't lie to me, would you, Rog?" I asked. "I mean, y'know, that old gag you guys were pulling, switching cute names on Carmel houses. This is not light stuff, my friend. And what the hell do you want me to do?"

"I don't know, Pat. I'm out of my league. But I'm afraid. I thought you . . . an investigator . . . could maybe snoop around a bit. Find out something. I surely don't want somebody to blow up the Sunset Center or the Mission."

I stared at him. Could I flat-out turn him down? Well, not really. "Roger, I'll do what I can, which may be nothing at all. I cannot imagine why anybody would try to screw up the Bach Festival. But . . . I'll do . . . what I can."

All this stuff was going through my mind when Reiko appeared in the doorway.

"Guess who's here," she said with a blinding grin that looked really painful.

"Go away, woman. Leave me in my blue funk."

"You'll be sorry. I'll just kick the bastard out, then."

"Wait, Reiko. I didn't mean it. Who's here?"

She stepped aside and revealed her visitor. My God! Carlos Vesper! A creature from the past. A champion con artist and flimflam man. A driver of Lamborghinis.

"Hi, Riordan," he said, and sat down on my hard and creaky visitor's chair.

2

"You got the Lamborghini back, right?"

CARLOS hadn't changed much. A few more lines, some gray hair. Maybe ten or fifteen pounds around the middle. He was smiling, obviously pleased that he had surprised the bejesus out of me simply by showing up in my life again.

"Hey, Riordan, you look shocked. Can't you just welcome an old friend?"

"Why are you here, Carlos? You were supposed to live happily ever after, married to Flo Grimme, the lady who believed you were an Indian guru named Maharishi Mehta. By the way, why did you take the name of a famous symphony conductor?"

"Liked his looks, Riordan. Big head, big face. Handsome devil."

Still puzzled and a little irritated, I relaxed a bit.

"So, Carlos, without doubt you have a very good reason for being here at this time in my life. The only reason I ever had to seek you out was when you were a sort of collateral suspect in a murder."

"Just visiting, my friend, just visiting. More or less."

Carlos was different, somehow. In the past he had seemed

alternately an aggressive blowhard and a scared rabbit. He had cheerfully taken many senior citizens of the Monterey Peninsula for thousands of dollars with his promises of great wealth to be had from investments in obscure start-up companies. Without the tiniest show of remorse, I might add.

When he turned up later, beturbaned, in dark makeup, posing as an Indian mystic, he pursued and won (or was dragooned by) the aforementioned Mrs. Grimme, who had shed several wealthy husbands and owned one of the ugliest mansions in Pebble Beach.

"I don't believe it, Carlos. You never come to me unless you want something. And I never come to you unless you've done something nasty to somebody."

"Flo died a year ago. I guess the news wasn't big enough for the *Herald* or the *Pine Cone*. One morning in Brunei—we were guests of the sultan—I rolled over and she was stone cold dead. Pity. Only seventy-five and in the prime of life." He paused and, rolling his eyes heavenward, made a clumsy attempt to cross himself. "Great old girl, Flo. Left me her entire fortune. You wouldn't believe, Riordan, you wouldn't believe."

"You got the Lamborghini back, right? You sold that piece of ridiculous architecture in Pebble Beach, right? You're living it up with a new chick every night."

"No, no, no, no, Riordan. I'm with the love of my life. Anastasia Hawkins, my dream girl. That's why I'm here. You remember her, don't you?"

"I do not, Carlos. And I didn't know you ever had a 'dream girl.' And I still think you are certifiable. Very greedy, amoral, and certifiable."

"You'll take that back when you understand. I owe you something, Pat. I'm not sure just what, but I owe you for not blowing my cover when I was conning, I mean courting Flo Grimme. Well, I'm not sure it'll be any help to you but there is a strong rumor that there's to be a disaster of sorts at the Bach Festival."

That stopped me cold. First Roger Carrington lays this Festival debacle on me and now Carlos Vesper backs it up. If I had heard it from Carlos first, I'd have dismissed it. But Carlos must have known something.

My face probably gave me away. I'm cursed with this face. It has an air of innocence and naïveté, and it gives me away every time. Lord, the many times I have wished for the chiseled features of Eastwood. The gift of non-expression. The sheer talent of being furious, amorous, shattered or terrified without giving oneself away.

Carlos grinned. "So I'll tell you about it. I see the veins pulsating in your temple, the color rising in your cheeks, your mouth hanging open. Gotcha this time, Riordan. A real good gotcha."

Reiko, who had been taking in this scene from the doorway finally spoke out in a voice like a samurai sword: "Get on with it, you miserable bastard, or get out. Cause any more trouble for my partner and I'll flip you out that window. It's only two stories, but it'll break you up pretty good."

"Okay, okay, " said Vesper. "You don't recognize the name of Anastasia Hawkins, my true love. It figures. She's the woman I took up with a while back when I had to leave the Peninsula. The cello player with the San Francisco Symphony. I fell in love with her knees. Remember?"

It came back to me then. Carlos had to get out of town in a hurry and bunked in for a while with the cellist. One night, he later told me, when she got out of bed to go the bathroom, he could not restrain himself from a remark, made, of course, in admiration and wonderment, about her bow legs—and she threw him out.

"You still look pretty disturbed, Pat. Listen. Anastasia is here rehearsing for the Bach Festival. There is a rumor making the rounds that one or more of the participants this year is a target. There's very little more than that. A rumor. But Annie thinks there's something to it. There's a lot of jealousy among musicians. Artists are like that, too. Temperamental, egotistical, bad-tempered. Annie thinks that maybe somebody who wasn't included—a conductor, maybe, or a second trombone— is just crazy enough to spoil the whole affair."

I was coming around. "Or guarantee the fact that when the word gets around nobody will come. It's an old ploy, Carlos. You don't have to have a real bomb threat to clear out Soldier Field or the L.A. Coliseum. Just so enough people believe it's real. Voilà, the plot's a success." I get a kick out of invoking Hercule Poirot upon occasion.

"Okay, Riordan. I told you what I heard. You're supposed to be wired into the law of Monterey County. I thought I could help you be a hero. You, know, like I owe you."

"Item one, I already heard some vague notion about trouble at the Bach Festival. Item two, I think it's just bullshit. Item three, it's the last place in the world for anything violent to happen. Music lovers are gentle people."

"Right," said Carlos. "Music lovers are gentle people. Musicians are not, necessarily. And I've lied to you just a little bit. My concern is mainly about Anastasia. I wouldn't want her to get caught up in a crossfire or blown up in the middle of a Vivaldi. I was hoping it wouldn't come to this, but I'll commission you to look after the love of my life."

3

"Bless you, Riordan, you won't regret this."

IT was hard for me to accept Carlos Vesper's referring to any woman as "the love of my life." I could not believe that Carlos had ever been unselfish enough to love anybody.

"This cellist—this Anastasia—she's obviously participating in the Bach Festival. Playing music?" I asked, covering my disbelief with absolute stupidity.

"Come on, Pat. She's a very good musician. She got the job with the San Francisco Symphony when she was barely twenty-two. Beat out thirty or forty other cellists. Of course she's playing. And I have become a lover of classical music. You have not lived if you have not heard the Goldberg Variations played by a virtuoso harpsichordist."

I stared at the man. Looked like Vesper. Sounded like Vesper. Somebody out there cloning Vespers? This lady cellist with the sexy knees must have hypnotized the guy.

"It is with pleasure . . . and . . . and humility that I accept your commission, Carlos. But I better talk to the lady in question. Where do I find her?"

"Bless you, Riordan. You won't regret this." He slipped a slim wallet out of his inside jacket pocket and withdrew from

it a sheaf of hundred dollar bills. He laid five of them on my
desk, neatly fanned. "This is a down payment. If all goes well,
you get another thou when this culture wallow is over. The
beautiful Anastasia and I are staying in a small rental house on
Lincoln Street in Carmel. I'm not sure why, but it has a peculiar sign on it, pink with purple lettering: 'Rising Gorge.'"

Ah, the White Knights at work again. Carrington's crew
took offense at some of the cutesy signs and ridiculous color
schemes of a lot of the houses in Carmel. Their mission is to
go out under cover of darkness and rename the more offensive
ones. It's easy with the rentals. Nobody ever even sees the signs
except the tenants, most of whom don't recognize the nasty
implications of the changes.

"Is she there now?" I asked.

"Of course not. She's rehearsing at the Sunset Center. Some
Beethoven, some Vivaldi, some other stuff."

"Carlos, why do they call it the Bach Festival if they let all
those other dead composers in?"

He looked like he was about to strike me, and I ducked
slightly. However, with admirable restraint, he only grasped
the edge of my desk and showed his excellent teeth (capped, I
think) in a mirthless grin.

"It has always been thus, infidel. It has always been mainly
Bach, with some other guys tossed in for variety. Do you get
that, dog of an unbeliever?"

"Hold it, Carlos. Those are Muslim curses, I believe.
Nothing you'd hear from an Indian mystic."

He seemed to relax a little. "Anastasia will be home this
evening. Come by about five. We'll have a drink and you can
get the scoop from her." He offered his hand rather limply and
I shook it without much confidence. I also picked up the
money and stuffed it into my pants pocket before he could get
it back. He tried to pat Reiko's ass as he went by her, but she
was too quick for him.

"What do you think, partner?" said Reiko.

"'Bout what?"

"The whole enchilada, pal. Two guys tell you about rumors

of violence during the Bach Festival. Ol' Carrington even
bought you a meal, you should live so long. I have a lot of
respect for Roger, but Carlos is still very weird. I asked you
what you think."

"I think . . . I think something's going to happen. God
knows what. What's that stuff violinists use on bows? Is it
resin or rosin?"

"It's both, you ninny. Rosin is resin. Only rosin is the stuff
you get after distilling turpentine."

"How'd you know that?"

"I looked it up. A long time ago. When I was taking violin
lessons. I might have been as good as Midori."

"You never told me that. About the violin."

"Why should I have? Besides, Midori is a kid and I'm
crashing into forty. She's good at the fiddle. I'm good at mar-
tial arts. Same thing."

Standing behind my chair, she put her arms around my
neck and kissed me on my bald spot.

"Reiko. Remember the night . . . the night we, ah, consummated our relationship?"

She made a loud noise, something between a scream and a
snort. "'Consummated'? Holy shit, Riordan, what century are
you livin' in? Nobody says that any more. Except maybe
lawyers and cops. Come off it. We went to bed together. It was
nice."

"You knew I didn't drink. You knew I was AA. Hadn't had
a drink for like ten or twelve years. And you gave me one of
those thimble cups of sake in what was the most elaborate
drinking ceremony of my career. You were trying to seduce
me, right? Didn't you realize that one little drink could have
been my downfall. If I didn't have a will of iron, I'd be
slumped on a bench down on the waterfront with a bottle of
Tokay in a paper bag."

She laughed loudly and insultingly. "'Downfall'? Patrick,
you are some kind of strange case. I believe the last 'downfall'
occurred in 1911. Like where this little girl tried to stop her
daddy at the door of the saloon. Listen, friend, the tiny cup of

sake I gave you was a goddam placebo. A little sweet non-alcoholic wine. I know you. I know how you feel about drinking. I was around when you got sober. Do you think I'd take a chance on sending you out into the saloons again? You were just ready to get it on with me, baby. Would I give you real sake? No, no, a thousand times no."

The last part she sang merrily, and skipped out the door.

4

"May I call you Annie?"

THE house on Lincoln street where Carlos and his Anastasia were living was a typical Carmel rental. It sat back on its narrow lot, approached by a snaky line of flagstones ending in a steep narrow staircase to a sort of mini-porch. From the street you get the impression that it's bigger than it is. I had been in it before when a dangerous lady stage director was the tenant. As I looked at the place from the street, I thought about that woman. She had come to Carmel to direct a play at the Forest Theater and had spent her leisure time trapping and seducing many of the eligible (and not so eligible) males in town. She even made a pass at me, believe it or not. But I turned her down.

Mounting the stairs to the front stoop, I flipped the brass knocker and hoped somebody inside would hear the tinny sound.

Almost immediately the door opened and there stood Anastasia Hawkins.

"Mr. Riordan, I presume. Carlos just went out for a bottle of wine. Should be back soon. Come in and sit down."

She surprised the daylights out of me. I'm not sure what I

expected. Some kind of self-possessed woman with a severe hairdo and a forbidding expression. Somebody I could match up with Carlos, maybe. What was I thinking? A female version of Carlos Vesper? I couldn't speak for a moment.

Anastasia Hawkins was a tallish, slenderish redhead with a model's figure. Her eyes were the color of the Pacific Ocean on a bright day. Her face was stunningly beautiful with little or no makeup.

I mumbled some sort of gibberish that was intended to express thanks for the invitation to enter and be seated. I entered and sat down. I smiled idiotically. You're expected to smile, aren't you, when a lady asks you to come in and sit down.

Anastasia smiled back, a little puzzled. "Carlos is so forgetful. Fifteen minutes ago he remembered that you were coming. Thought he simply had to dash out for wine. I'm sorry."

I had recovered from my initial shock by this time, so I said: "Actually, it's you I've come to see. Carlos knows that. I'm sure you know that he came to my office to engage me to investigate some hot rumor that there's to be trouble at the Bach Festival. Probably a lot of nonsense, don't you think?"

Her smile vanished. "No. There is talk among the musicians. I've heard it from several sources. No details, no particulars. Just trouble. Trouble that can be damaging. Or fatal."

I studied the woman's face. It was hard not to study the woman's face. Staring at her kind of put my mind off track. I heard what she said, but I was so fascinated by her face that it barely registered. What she said, that is.

"Carlos calls you Annie. May I call you Annie?"

I do believe she blushed. "Of course. Everybody does."

I took a deep breath. "Annie, last night a friend of mine, a prominent senior citizen with a keen interest in the Bach Festival, told me about the rumors. He's worried sick. But I, a very unmusical type, am used to hearing a lot of weird stuff. People come to me usually because something has already happened. Or they want to get some dirt on somebody. It's the nature of my business. I don't do a lot of mysterious threat work. Mainly I handle routine investigations for corporations, research work for lawyers, unfriendly divorces. But since Rog Carrington is a friend and Carlos is what you might call an old acquaintance, I've agreed to find out whatever I can. Mind you, I've known your boyfriend quite a while and although I like him in spite of myself, he has a spotty reputation."

"I know," said Anastasia. "He's told me about some of his misadventures. I'm sure you remember how he and I first met. He used to come to the symphony concerts in San Francisco as escort for one of the richest widows in the city. There are a lot of those, Mr. Riordan. By the way, may I call you Pat?"

I nodded and grinned my idiot grin. My eyes were beginning to water.

She continued: "After Carlos had been to a number of concerts he somehow got hold of my phone number and called. You'll never believe this but he told me I had the most beautiful knees he'd ever seen." She blushed again, much redder than before. "Can you imagine? I'd never heard of beautiful knees. I don't think knees are very pretty at all. Do you?" She pulled up her skirt which was already at mid-thigh and glanced coyly at her knees. They were, indeed, some classy knees.

"Yeah," I said. "I would concur with Carlos's judgment. Although I ain't exactly a connoisseur of patellas, I must comment that yours are rather compelling."

She laughed. "You're funny, Pat. But about Carlos. He was living with me in my San Francisco apartment and we were quite happy together. Until one night I got out of bed to go to the bathroom—we always slept in the nude, you know—and he made that crude remark about my bowlegs. I've been aware of them for a long time. They're really not that bad, although I used to wear floppy slacks a lot because of remarks I got when I was a kid. But when Carlos. . . ." She frowned. "I told him to pack and get out as fast as he could.

"But I never could get him out of my mind. I lost track of him. I didn't know about his marriage to that rich old woman in Pebble Beach. But when he called me after his return from Brunei and told me he was still in love with me, I asked him to come back, in spite of everything. We've been very happy again. I know it's chancey, but I really don't care. If he's conning me, I say so be it!" At that moment the door opened and Vesper came in waving a large wine bottle. "Hey, Riordan, you beat me to it, did you. How's about a glass of this very rare French Colombard from Ernie and Julio?"

"You forget, Carlos. I can't take the stuff, " I said.

"Christ, man, this is just a little white wine, maybe ten or eleven percent. This ain't booze."

"Been there. Done that. Forget it, Carlos."

He looked at me a little cross-eyed. I know the look. Carlos had been into the sauce since lunch. Happens sometimes when a guy is too rich to have anything to do.

Anastasia was embarrassed. She knew the guy had a heat on, as we used to say in San Francisco. She didn't try to cover up. "Carlos just sits around when I'm working, Pat. I wish I could get him interested in some kind of hobby. He's a little old to take up surfing. He plays golf, but can't go more than nine holes without gasping for breath."

"He might take up a musical instrument. Couldn't hurt. He could lift a flute or maybe a piccolo. But I guess he hasn't enough wind. Percussion, maybe. Tympani or triangle."

Carlos was slumped on the couch with his eyes closed. In minutes he began to snore.

I asked Anastasia: "Does he always do that?"

"Well, not always." She took an afghan from the back of couch and tenderly spread it over her snoozing lover.

We sat in silence for a while. It's like I couldn't think of anything to say and Anastasia was trying to compose some statement in her mind.

Finally, she spoke: "Pat, I know you're probably wondering why I'm so attached to this man, this very strange man. He's only as honest as he has to be. He's not the handsome demigod I dreamed of and he drinks too much. My God, I'm about to break into "My Bill" from *Showboat*. I don't have an explanation. I guess it's just that I've been in love with music since I was eight years old. The men I'd known were all musicians.

Passionate . . . but only about their art. I had no idea that anybody would find me attractive. I play the cello. I'm not Yo Yo
Ma, but I'm a pretty damn good cellist.

"And then along came Carlos, who was in love with my
knees. At first I thought it was funny. But when I got to know
the man, I found it rather sweet. He seemed really to love me.
And naïve little girl that I was, I fell in love with him."

Carlos was snoring loudly. I reached over and thumped him
a couple of times until he snorted moistly and began to breathe
normally. His mouth hung open and the folds of his ample
neck were multiplied under his chin. I had a quick flash of
what Carlos Vesper would look like when he got older and I
shuddered slightly.

I turned my attention to Anastasia. "What's all this about,
anyhow? Why would any living soul want to raise hell with
the Bach Festival?"

Annie looked at me with a directness I hadn't seen before.
"I haven't told Carlos but I think I know. It's Mischa. Mischa
and Theodore. They have hated each other with a passion for
a long, long time. They're here now, and will be to the end in
August.

5

Pity, I don't look like Newman.

WHEN I got home after that mystical session with Anastasia Hawkins, I sat down in my big chair with the ottoman and tried to think.

Annie and I had managed with considerable effort to get Carlos into bed. We didn't even try to undress him, just loosened his tie and took off his shoes. The man must weigh two-forty or thereabouts. During the operation I felt that sharp little pain in my lower back that tells me that I am physically beyond the pale. I said goodbye to the lovely cellist and told her I'd call when I got anything.

It was a meager beginning. Mischa Bialystock, Annie told me, had been for many years first violin in a string quartet which was to be featured at the Bach Festival. Unhappily, people had been saying that Mischa had lost it. His fingering was sloppy, his tone thin. There were even those who said that Mischa played flat. Principal among the man's critics was Theodore Blum, a conductor whose job it was to select some of the artists to perform at the Festival.

Although Theodore could not pass over Mischa's string quartet, he suffered its presence with a grand hauteur, and placed it whenever possible in the most obscure venues. Mischa ignored Theodore and Theodore did not admit the very existence of Mischa. The men were thrown together season after season at musical events in both hemispheres from a date that Anastasia was much too young to remember. The venomous attitude of each toward the other had grown worse over the decades, although it was generally considered a fact that neither man could quite remember how it started.

It's not that there was every any thing physical. Neither man was particularly large or muscular. One could imagine a face-slapping or some such contact, but never had it occurred, at least in public.

However, Anastasia told me, several of the participants in the Bach Festival had reported to her that they had heard Mischa, in a fit of anger, swearing that sooner or later he was going to kill Theodore. Moreover, he said he had studied just the proper method, and that nobody would ever know who did it.

Knowing that Mischa tended to be emotional and very much aware of his loss of the ability to make his Stradivarius sing, people who heard the threats shrugged them off. But the man continued to make them, aloud and always in the presence of those he knew would spread the word.

I became aware that I was talking to myself. This is a very bad sign.

I stood up, trying to decide whether to walk to the kitchen and make myself a peanut butter and jelly sandwich, or drive down to the Bully III for a slab of prime rib.

Alone. I really don't like being alone, although I've lived that way for a long time. How long? Maybe fourteen years since Helen, my only wife so far, was killed. It wasn't a criminal act that took her away. It was some bastard who crossed the center line at eighty miles an hour and smashed us head on. I got some bumps and cuts. Helen died. And I have lived alone.

Funny thing about it is that I'm the kind of guy who really shouldn't live by himself. I had that woman named Sally

Morse who used to warm my bed from time to time. But she wouldn't live with me. Now it's Reiko, whom I have loved since I first saw her, but she won't move in. Doesn't help my self-esteem much.

But I am a sexagenarian. Look it up. It ain't a disease, but it might as well be. What it means is that I have lived more years than I want to admit. I'm reminded of the wonderful advice of Satchel Page: "Don't look back. Somethin' might be gainin' on you."

Hell, look at Paul Newman. Still kickin' it around and havin' a wonderful time. Pity I don't look like Newman.

But I'm drifting. I do this often. You can always skip a few paragraphs to get to the important stuff.

What was I supposed to do? First positive thing I did on this mission was to call Rog Carrington.

When he answered, I said: "Got some stuff for you. About that matter we discussed at dinner."

"Good, Pat, good. Do you know what's going to happen and who's involved?"

"Well, no. Let me ask you a couple of questions. You know about a couple of guys named Mischa Bialystock and Theodore Blum?"

There was a pause and a sharp intake of breath at the other end. "Those two? You must be kidding, Pat. Those guys have been at it for years. Lightweights! No way either on of 'em could do any harm. They glare at each other. They malign each other every chance they get, but neither one could fight his way out of a girls' glee club with an Uzi. Forget it, son."

"All I know is what Anastasia Hawkins told me. She seems to think. . . ."

"Forget it, Riordan. She's a child. Fantastic cello, but a child. You might better spend your time with Evan Schmidt."

"Who's Evan Schmidt?"

"Just ask around. You'll find out." He wasn't being much help at all and he hung up abruptly.

6

"You know Schmidt?"

"BIALYSTOCK and Blum?" Reiko seemed agitated. "You're kidding, right? Somebody's pulling your leg."

"Whatever are you talking about, " I asked in all innocence.

"Don't those names mean anything to you, smart guy? Haven't you heard them before?"

"I don't think so."

"Dammit, Riordan, they're the two idiot musicians who walked off Letterman one night. Neither one knew that the other was supposed to appear. One of 'em came on first and was sitting down when the other one came in. They looked at each other and went off in different directions. Dave just sat there with that dumb gap-toothed smile on his face. Nobody said anything for a whole minute until Marlo Thomas burst out laughing like crazy. She was already on, see, when it happened and she and Dave just laughed like hyenas. Hardly got through the rest of the show. Every time they seemed to settle down they'd laugh up a storm. It was a riot!"

"Sorry, kid. You gotta understand. Before you started spending the night now and then, I went to bed early. Nobody has kept me up since Carson. Or was it Steve Allen?"

"You're givin' yourself away, boy. When you go back that far you're really tired. I don't like to remind you but I've got to. You told me a long time ago that you didn't want to hear about age."

I looked very closely at my sansei partner. Damned if I could see that she looked like ten or more years had passed since I first saw her. Maybe a few gray strands in her black hair, maybe a couple of lines at the corners of her eyes, but that's it. She was sitting as usual on a corner of my desk, swinging her legs so that they made muffled thumps in a steady rhythm. I had asked her not to wear heels around the office, although at five-foot-nothin' she did look a little taller in them. But I couldn't stand the staccato crack of heels on the bare wooden floor. It was one of my few triumphs with Reiko.

"Carrington has told me that I have to ask around about a character named Evan Schmidt. Ever hear of him?" I asked.

She shook her head. "Face it, pal. I am a know-nothing when it comes to the Bach Festival. Classical music in general leaves me cold, although I do like 'Un Bel Di' from *Madama Butterfly*. Always makes me cry."

"You identify. I can see that," I said. "But it's *Madame Butterfly*, isn't it?

"Shows how much you think you know. It's Italian, buddy. *Madama* is what it says on the libretto."

"Thought you didn't know anything about classical music."

"One opera. That's it. Poor little geisha screwed by an American sailor. I'd castrate the bastard."

"Whoa, there, Reiko-san. It's fiction."

She pouted and muttered something under her breath that I didn't quite hear and didn't want to.

"Do me a favor, little one," I said in my oiliest manner. "Get on the phone with anybody you know who's connected with the Bach Festival, and see what you can find out about Evan Schmidt. I'd be ever so much obliged." I tried to sound like Scarlett O'Hara in that last sentence, but I think I came off Lyndon Johnson.

She left the room trying to make as much noise as possible with her soft slip-on shoes.

In spite of my objections to the expense, we now have two phone lines coming into the office. Reiko needed to use our old line for her Internet machinations, and the damn thing was always busy. When she wasn't e-mailing her relatives in Osaka, she was yakking with one of her female friends. Finally we got the second line. Even now, though, she's probably plotting to take it over.

So, while Reiko was calling anybody she knew who was remotely concerned about the Bach Festival, I put in a call to my friend Armand Colbert, oenophile, restaurateur, entrepreneur extraordinaire. If anybody can get inside dope on anything in Carmel, it's Armand. He invited me over for a cup of coffee and a croissant.

I use any excuse to get out of the office. It's not that Reiko makes me uncomfortable. Inferior, sometimes, but not uncomfortable. I drove over to Armand's restaurant in Carmel.

After the usual exchange of warmest greetings, I said: "Armand, you're a man of many interests. What do you know about the Bach Festival?"

"It happens every year, I know that. Late July, early August. Anything else?"

"That's not quite what I meant. Do you go? Are you a music fan?"

"Of course I'm a music fan. No, I don't go. I take that back. I went once. " He chuckled. "Maybe I should have said, 'I take that Bach.'"

I laughed a little just to be polite. "Do you know anybody connected with the Festival?"

"Not really. That is, not really any of promoters. I know lots of the local folks who go every year. They all eat here. Not all my business is tourist, you know."

I figured I had reached a dead end. But I had to try one last thing. "Armand, have you ever heard of guy named Evan Schmidt?"

Silence. Then: "Why do you ask?"

"Roger Carrington told me to seek out Evan Schmidt. It's part of an investigation. Not much of a deal. You know Schmidt?"

Armand spoke slowly, as though he needed to be absolutely accurate in what he was saying: "I have met the man. He is a music critic from San Francisco. He used to have a small get-away house on Perry Newberry Street, but he sold it a few years back. He eats here when he's in town. I really cannot tell you any more. Your coffee all right? Need it heated up?"

That ended the conversation. Armand was summoned from my presence by one of those willowy hostesses he always seems to have in his restaurant. I sat alone, staring a a cold cup of Armand's bad coffee.

He'd never brushed me off like that before. The man has always been a reliable source for any and all information about anything going on in or around the city of Carmel-by-the-Sea. But he really buttoned up when I mentioned Schmidt.

I walked out into the bright sunlight and squinted badly until I remembered to put on my dark glasses. One of these days I'm gonna get bifocals. The kind that change color in the sun. Don't need anything but the lower part, you know. But I hate to have to fuss with sun glasses. And if I wear 'em indoors I bump into things.

For those who've never experienced the Central Coast area of California, a word of advice. In midsummer it can be pretty cold and damp, like it says in "The Lady is a Tramp." Fog is the name of the game. When it's sunny and warm today, you can bet your ass it's gonna be foggy and cold tomorrow. But most elsewhereans learn to love it.

A guy named Schmidt. Not your most frightening name. Music critic from San Francisco. Critics are guys who don't do anything all that well, but are somehow qualified to judge the work of others.

I decided to go back to my office on Alvarado Street in Monterey and call a friend of mine on the *Herald,* the only daily newspaper game in town. It's pretty sad about newspapers. They're suffering a slow and painful death. On any given morning, I can go through the *Herald* in five minutes. Then I do the "Jumble" and keep the TV program. Sad.

Reiko was gone when I got back to the office. I glanced at the digital clock on her desk: 12:15. Lunch time. My contact from the newspaper was out. I left a message on her voice-mail and started out the door to get my own lunch when the phone rang.

"Riordan and Masuda," I said, cheerfully. "Can we help you?"

"To whom am I speaking?" said a voice in some sort of affected Mayfair accent.

"This whom is Pat Riordan. Whom are you?"

"My name is Theodore Blum. Word has reached me that you are investigating a rumor involving the Bach Festival. I think we need to talk."

Well, I thought. Well, well. "Any time, maestro. You name it."

"Two o'clock this afternoon. My room. The Pine Inn."

"I'll be there," I said, and hung up.

7

"A dead body, ma'am."

IT seems that I'm always making trips back and forth between Monterey and Carmel. It's not that it's all that far. Never clocked it, really. I find my car somewhere around one or two blocks (if I'm lucky, I don't have a parking ticket), run up to Pacific and out to Munras via Soledad. The Highway One freeway ends at the top of Carmel Hill, and you're practically there. Ten, fifteen minutes, thereabouts, from my office on Alvarado Street.

I grabbed a quick sandwich at Stravaganza, a place down at the Crossroads Shopping Center that I favor. There was a little time left before I had to encounter Theodore Blum at the Pine Inn, so I drove up to the parking lot at the beach near the mouth of the Carmel River, sat in the car and watched the Pacific Ocean. I meditated. I do this a lot. Meditation, that is. Rest my eyes. Too often fall asleep. Sound of the surf, smell of the sea air, you know.

Time passed. I paid no attention. Then, the sudden realization that I had an appointment. I fished out my little half-glasses so I could see my wrist watch. Five minutes 'til two. Another reason I've gotta get bifocals. I must have lost fifteen seconds looking for those damn little glasses. Oughta get a digital with numerals a half-inch high. Damn!

I found a parking space on Sixth, back of the Pine Inn. You can't imagine what a coup that is in the tourist-clogged streets of Carmel in midsummer.

As I crossed the street to the narrow passage that leads to the hotel entrance, I remembered that the Pine Inn is one of only two institutions here when I first walked down Ocean Avenue in the early fifties. The other is the Mediterranean Market. Everything else is different. Not better, just different.

I checked the desk for the location of Blum's room and was given directions. The Pine Inn is not quite like regular hotels, with elevators and the like. I walked out the back door to an extension of the main building and found Blum's room up a flight of stairs. I knocked.

Nothing happened. Didn't hear a sound. Door didn't open. I knocked again, a little louder. Still zip.

I checked the room number. Right one. Ah, well, the guy's a musician, right? Absent minded. Forgot the whole thing. Goddam stick-waving megalomaniac! I was very angry at that moment. As a last resort, I tried the doorknob. The door opened with the long penetrating sigh of rusty hinges, common in the year-round dampness of Carmel.

At first the room seemed empty. I stood in the doorway, uncertain. Had I just broken and entered? Is that a felony? Maybe I ought to just beat it.

But there was something strange here. Everything seemed neatly in order, but there was a huge lump on the bed. Gingerly I lifted the quilted bedspread to uncover the body of what must once have been Theodore Blum. Quickly, I checked his vital signs. I learned how to do this by watching hospital shows on TV.

As you may have surmised, the guy was dead. Not a mark on him that I could see, but dead, nevertheless. He was lying prone with his face turned to one side, his eyes wide open.

I found a chair and slumped into it. Okay, next move. Call the cops. Why am I here? They don't get too many murders in

Carmel, so how're they going to react? Especially, they don't get murders in the Pine Inn. I was a little miffed when they put in another Italian restaurant, like we need another Italian restaurant in this town. But why am I sitting here bitching about an Italian restaurant when there's a dead man lying there four feet from me?

As I remember it now, it couldn't have been more than a few minutes until I picked up the phone and dialed 911. Time, the fourth dimension, has a way of compressing or expanding according to the events at hand. I told the policewoman who answered the phone that I had found a corpse at the Pine Inn.

"A what?" she said, stunned.

"A dead body, ma'am. I think it's a man named Theodore Blum but I'm not sure because I've never really seen Theodore Blum."

"Who are you?" A natural question.

"Pat Riordan, ma'am. I'm a citizen. I live here. Is Captain Miller around?"

"Who?"

"Miller. Captain. Big guy. You know him." I was a bit frustrated.

"Oh. I'll send someone right away. What room?"

I gave her the number, hung up the phone and flopped down in the chair again to stare at the lump on the bed.

Maybe natural causes. Guy's quite a bit overweight, I'd judge. Heart problem or stroke, maybe. Sonofabitch! Why do I have to be the one to find him? What did he want to talk to me about, anyway?

Answers came there none, in the words of the immortal Peter Cooke to Dudley Moore, and in time came heavy footfalls on the stairs.

Two uniformed policemen came into the room, looked at Blum on the bed, and then looked at me. Their heads seemed perfectly synchronized as they turned back to the maestro's corpse. Then one of them moved in to examine the body. The other approached me.

"You Riordan?" he asked.

"Me Riordan, yeah," I said, wishing I hadn't tried to be so goddam clever.

"What's the story, Riordan? You kill this guy?"

"No, I did not kill this guy. He was dead when I came in. No visible marks, although I did not strip the body to see if there was a hole in him anywhere. No blood around. The man appears to have died of natural causes, whatever that means."

The officer looked at me doubtfully, but said no more.

I asked him: "Who's going to investigate? I know a couple of policemen in Carmel."

"Don't know. Hell, Riordan, we just got here. I don't even know if this guy's still warm. Is he still warm, Harry?"

Harry felt Blum's face. "Warmish. Guess he hasn't been dead long."

"I'll vouch for that," I said. "The guy called me about twelve-fifteen and asked me to meet him here at two o'clock. He couldn't have been dead long."

All our heads turned at a choking sound from the direction of the door. A man stood there clutching the door jamb. His face was ashen and his knees sagged.

"Who are you, sir?" asked one of the cops.

"My name . . . my name is Mischa Bialystock."

8

"He's the killer?"

THE man sagged to his knees in slow motion, froze in the kneeling position and stared at the body on the bed.

The first cop turned to me. "Who the hell is he?"

"A first violin. Sworn enemy of the deceased, as I get it. Mischa Bialystock."

"You know him?"

"Never laid eyes on him before."

"Then how do you know who he is?"

He had me there. For a second I could not remember how I recognized the man. Intuition, maybe. He just looked like a Russian first violinist should look. Besides, he announced himself when he appeared in the door. "Maybe," I said, "because he told us who he was."

"Oh, yeah," said the officer.

The other cop, Harry, helped Bialystock up and sat him in a chair. The man sat with his hands in his lap and his head bowed so his chin was on his chest. I could hear his raspy breathing. His face was wet with sweat.

Pretty soon there were all sorts of people in the room. More cops, a detective, paramedics, hotel people. It was a sort

of macabre version of the Marx Brothers and everybody else in
the tiniest stateroom on an ocean liner.

"What do they think they're doing?" I asked the first cop,
whose name he had told me was Virgil. "They ain't gonna
revive that guy. He's ready for the box."

"Standard procedure. They've got to check him out for
vitals. Dead or not, they have to be satisfied."

"Ever see anybody that dead come back to life?"

Virgil gave me a withering look. "Standard procedure,
dammit. They got a bunch of thing they have to do with a pre-
sumed dead body. Then we wait 'til the coroner's office sends
somebody."

"Riordan! " A voice behind me so close that it set my ears
ringing.

I turned to face Eddie Marovich, a detective I had known
for most of the ten years I had lived on the Monterey
Peninsula. Eddie and I had bumped heads before but we never
seemed to see eye-to-eye.

"Hi, Eddie, long time no . . ."

"Doin' your Jessica Fletcher act again. Turnin' up with the
deceased in a murder case. You psychic or somethin'?"

"Eddie, it doesn't need to be murder. Yet. It's a dead body.
Guy was here for the Bach Festival. He's a conductor. Look at
him. No holes, no blood. Maybe a heart attack. On the other
hand, maybe some exotic poison that leaves no traces in the
bloodstream. It's your baby, pal. You figure it out."

"Find a place to park, Riordan. Wait a minute. Who's the
weirdo in the chair?"

"His name is Bialystock. He's a first violin. He and the guy
on the bed were sworn enemies."

Marovich's eyes bulged and his face reddened. "He's the
killer?"

"You know, Eddie, that's a damn good idea. Better ask
him."

I've got to apologize here. I was being a smartass. I knew
Marovich as a very competent investigator, even though he
professed little respect for me. As a matter of fact the most

complimentary thing he had ever said about me was, "The sonofabitch shoulda been a lawyer." Or maybe that's not complimentary.

A couple of hours went by until all the proper people had come and gone including the coroner's men with the body bag. The mortal remains of Theodore Blum would be hauled over to the new morgue in Salinas and autopsied. Medical people would determine the exact cause of death, and all would be cool.

Finally, only Marovich and I were left. Both of us stood for a few minutes, just staring at the bed. With a long sigh, he turned to me.

"Okay, what's it all about? You tell me the dead guy called you and asked you to come up here. You came. Why?"

I told him most of what I knew. About the long-time feud between Bialystock and Blum. For some reason that I couldn't quite explain, I withheld the information about the possible disaster at the Bach Festival. Maybe this was it. Maybe it had already happened. No point in shakin' a lot of other people up.

"So the little guy—the weirdo—is our prime suspect. Looks like an easy one. Unless you offed whatsisname yourself."

"You're kidding, right? No motive. There is not one reason in this world that I would knock off a conductor. Unless, of course, he screwed up the B-Minor Mass."

With a look of supreme disgust, the detective started to leave.

"You'll be available, won't you, Riordan. I mean, we might need you for something. God knows I hope not, but we might."

"You have but to summon me. I think somebody at your place has my office number."

When Marovich was gone I looked around the room. It was, indeed, a room. A hotel room. Nothing to distinguish it from a million other hotel rooms, except it was older. I surprised myself by whistling a happy tune as a I went down the stairs and into the open courtyard. It was good to breathe the fresh air.

9

"Is Mr. Schmidt expecting you?"

"YOU are really some kind of dipshit, Riordan." Reiko was furious, as only she can be on too many occasions. It was the morning after the incident with the deceased Blum, and I had just related the details to her.

"He called me. He told me to meet him. I . . . well, I didn't meet him. He was dead, or that wasn't Blum on the bed. Or . . ."

"You should never have gone to his room. He might have been waiting for you to blast you!"

"Kid, you're crazy. Why would the guy want to get rid of me? I don't know anything."

"He might have thought you did!" I could see she was close to tears.

I put my arms around her and held her tight. She really would miss me if I got killed. That was somehow comforting. She sniffled and wiped her nose on my shirt.

"Guess maybe I overreacted," she said. "You're a trial, Riordan, but you're my trial."

She moved to her desk, snatched a tissue from the ever-present box and mopped her face. I grabbed another and wiped my shirt. Court will come to order.

Now perfectly in command, she told me what she had accomplished while I was occupied with the corpse of Theodore Blum.

"I checked with The Herald to see if anybody knew about Evan Schmidt," she said. "Sure, they told me. Hot shot critic from San Francisco. Used to work for the *Chronicle*, but got too controversial even for them. Free-lances now, for the most part, although he has a syndicated weekly column in about three hundred newspapers. Does magazine articles. Even in the *New Yorker*." She said that last in a kind of awe-struck voice. I have long been a subscriber to that magazine and have been watching it slowly sliding into high fashion. I mourn the deaths of Harold Ross and William Shawn. But I'm an old guy.

"Schmidt comes here every year for the Bach Festival," she went on. "He's here now, even though it hasn't begun yet. My contact at the *Herald* was sorta noncommittal, but I got the idea that nobody likes the man. Matter of fact, he's pretty generally considered a supercilious horse's ass who doesn't know Gustav Mahler from Norman Mailer. Well, that's extreme. But he's pretty good on seventeenth- and eighteenth-century guys. And modern atonalists. Get that? Atonalists! Composers who write music that ain't music. Like the three-note virtuosos of Rock, baby. Like Rap, where all you need is a drum!"

She was pretty vehement. "Reiko, my love, you are on the verge of being politically incorrect," I said, as gently as possible.

"I've got a right to be, dammit. I'm a minority!"

"Not with me, honey. Now, let's put aside these little diversions and get to the meat of the matter. Where is this arbiter of bad taste staying whilst here on the beautiful Monterey Peninsula?"

"At the Plaza on Cannery Row. Wanted to be near the Aquarium, I guess. Likes fish, maybe. Or to be as aloof as possible from what's going on in Carmel."

I glanced at Reiko's clock. "It is now five after ten. Let us proceed to the Row to pay a visit to the illustrious Schmidt."

That was either Poirot or Sherlock Holmes, I think. But the name of the mysterious music critic wouldn't be "Schmidt." Something more euphonious, like Walter de la Mare or that ilk. Boy, if I had been Conan Doyle, I would have produced some real thrillers, believe me. There are no good revelation scenes in modern crime fiction.

When I remembered where I parked my car, it was close to ten-thirty. We arrived at the Plaza at ten-forty-five. I have no idea why I'm being so specific about these times.

"Mr. Schmidt, please. Evan Schmidt," I said to the room clerk. Holy shit, it was the same clerk I had approached years ago when I was looking for a guy named Edgar Vanderhof. But that's a whole other story. The clerk was just as officious as he had been. It surprised me to find him because these people are gypsies and never stay in one place very long. All the hotels and motels on the Peninsula are advertising daily for room clerks, as well as maids and sundry other help. It's my hobby. Reading "Help Wanted." Don't know why.

"Is Mr. Schmidt expecting you?" Same old question.

"Well, no. We just thought we might catch him in." Same old answer.

Suspicious look from clerk. "I'll ring his room. Who shall I say is calling?"

"Mr. Riordan and Miss Masuda."

The clerk stroked his mustache with a long, tapered, exquisitely manicured index finger and gingerly picked up the phone as though the instrument might carry the germs of several strange tropical diseases. He turned his back on us.

We couldn't hear any of the conversation, but eventually the man gracefully returned the phone to its cradle and (I've got to say this) pirouetted to face us.

"Mr. Schmidt is in 327. He says he'll receive you." His nostrils quivered as though he had just caught the aroma of decaying sea creatures. He waved us toward the stairs and busied himself at the desk.

10

"My God, I never thought Mischa would go that far."

THE door of 327 opened to our first knock. Evan Schmidt stood looking at us through heavy black- rimmed glasses. He was as wide as the door and approximately twice as high as he was wide. He had an enormous mop of jet black hair and a matching beard. Both, I noted, were dyed. You can tell, see, when there's no variation in the color. Elementary. Reiko taught me that.

Schmidt had a voice that matched his size: "Do I know you? I really don't think so. When that damn clerk called I had a notion that Miss Masuda was one of those awful Japanese fiddlers they keep sending over nowadays." He looked at Reiko. "Are you a fiddler, girl?"

"I am a woman, sir, not a girl. I am not a violinist, although I could probably have been the best goddam violinist in the world if I hadn't busted the thing over the head of some clown who was trying to feel me up. " She stretched to her maximum height, which was about a quarter of an inch over five feet.

Schmidt burst out laughing. His laugh was like everything

else about him: loud, big, dynamic. For a moment I thought the pressure of the sound might blow the two of us down the hall. He laughed so hard he shook, and everything seemed to shake with him, even us. His face turned purple, he choked, he wheezed, and continued to laugh. Finally, with a prodigious effort, he stopped. "Come in, come in. I have no idea who you are or what you want, but I cannot resist a lady who would defend herself with a violin." He moved out of the doorway, and, with a sweeping gesture, bowed to Reiko.

Schmidt produced a rather soiled handkerchief and wiped the tears from his eyes as he retreated into the room. He sat on a couch and his bulk made it impossible for us to join him. He lit a very large cigar. Reiko looked at me with fire in her eyes. She and I stood for a moment, not knowing quite what to do.

"Sit down! Couple of chairs over there. Other side of the bed. I asked for a suite, but they didn't have one. Get the chairs."

Obediently, I got a chair and carried it to a position opposite the critic. I started after the other chair, but Reiko pushed me out of the way and got it herself. We sat and stared at Schmidt, and he stared back.

"All right, what are you? Reporters? Celebrity hounds? I never give autographs. Bill collectors?"

Reiko spoke: "We're private investigators. An interested party has commissioned us to investigate rumors of some sort of impending disaster which may or may not occur at the Bach Festival. Since you're such a big wheel, we thought maybe you could enlighten us."

"Ridiculous! This is one of the blandest, tamest gigs in the world. Believe me. Whatever you heard, it's all bullshit."

"Mr. Schmidt, have you heard about the death of Theodore Blum?" I asked.

That got a reaction. The critic was visibly shaken. It was as if I had told him that the entire New York Philharmonic had been killed in an air crash. Reiko took advantage of the moment, jumped from her chair, seized the man's cigar and dashed to the bathroom to flush it down the toilet. He didn't even seem to notice.

"Teddy? No. My God, I never thought Mischa would go that far. I knew they were both going to be here, but that feud of theirs had gotten to be all sham. I think by this time they had both completely forgotten what started it. But it was a good show, so they kept it up."

"You're speaking of Bialystock, right? You think he killed Blum? Wrong. From what I saw, the man died of what doctors refer to as 'natural causes.' I couldn't see a mark on him, " I said.

"You couldn't? How were you involved?"

"I found the body," I said. "Blum had called me at my office and asked me to come to his hotel room. I went. He was dead. That's all there is."

"It wasn't Mischa, then. I never thought he could kill anybody. It's good to hear."

"Well, the body hasn't been autopsied yet. Who knows what they'll find."

Schmidt looked at me, frowning. The man's eyebrows were magnificent. They were big and bushy, same color as the hair. He could manipulate them all over his forehead. When he heard about Blum, they jumped almost to his hairline. Now they shrouded his eyes.

"I didn't much like Teddy, but I respected him. He was a top flight organizer, an administrator. Learned it from Bernstein."

Reiko made a shrill noise and blurted: "Leonard Bernstein? He knew Leonard Bernstein?"

"No, little lady, Max Bernstein. When he was in the garment business. Who the hell do you think I meant? Lenny Bernstein! Teddy knew him when it was 'steen,' not 'stine.' Lenny's dead, you know."

She sat back, properly chastened.

Apropos of nothing, I said, "Friend of mine in the army was a great buddy of Leonard Bernstein. The guy married a movie star, and—"

Reiko hissed: "Shut up, Riordan. That's a bunch of crap."
But it was true.
I could feel that we were drifting away from the subject of
Blum's death. "Mr. Schmidt," I said, "how well did you know
Bialystock?"
"Mischa? Like a brother. Sweetest guy in the world.
Couldn't harm a fly. Great tragedy, Mischa. All of us thought
he'd be another Isaac Stern. But he lost it, he lost it."
"What do you mean?" asked Reiko.
"It happens sometimes. A guy can be a budding virtuoso.
Then he loses it."
I cleared my throat. "What is 'it' that he loses?"
"Hard to tell. I've known string players who developed
arthritis in the left hand, couldn't manage the fingers. With
others I think it must have been something in the nervous sys-
tem. With Mischa, I just don't know."
"He still plays," said Reiko. "Wouldn't whatever he's lost
affect his performance with the quartet?"
"Not necessarily. Sometimes a fiddler who can play like
Perlman with an orchestra or a quartet cannot do it by himself. It's a mystery. If I had the answer, they'd all be concert-
masters."
I decided that we had unearthed all the useless material we
could get out of Evan Schmidt. "Well, we thank you, sir, for
receiving us. Would it be possible to talk to you again, in the
event that something comes up that you might be able to help
us with?"
"Sure. But call before you come. I'll be going over to
Carmel for the next few days to catch some rehearsals. Got to
get some background material." He looked at his hand as if he
was wondering what the hell happened to his cigar.
We started to leave.
"Be sure to bring the little Japanese fiddler woman with
you, pal. I might want to chase her around the room a little."
He started to laugh again. Same loud and dynamic laugh. I can
hear it now.
A sudden thought struck me. So help me it was like one of

those scenes in "Columbo." I wasn't chewing a cigar, nor was I wearing a raincoat, but the effect must have been the same.

I turned to Schmidt: "Just one more thing, if you please, sir. Are you aware of any physical problems that Mr. Blum might have had? How was his health, as far as you know?"

"Teddy had some sort of heart problem. I don't know what. I do know he had a pacemaker."

"Thank you," I said. "You've been very helpful." I gave him a soft salute, and turned to the door.

He hadn't been much help, I thought, but I was wrong.

11

"Looks like nobody did it."

DETECTIVE Marovich called me the next day. "Just thought you'd like to know. Post-mortem shows elevated alcohol but not enough to kill the guy. No drugs. No poisons. Medical examiner says his heart stopped. That's what kills most of us, I guess. Heart stops, guy checks out."

"Was it a heart attack? A massive coronary? What?"

"Doc says no heart attack. Blum had a pacemaker implant. Could be the thing failed."

"Are they going to test it. I mean, can you test it?

"I dunno. Up to the M.E., I guess."

"Thanks, Eddie, " I said, and hung up.

Reiko stuck her head in the door. "Any brilliant ideas, pal?" She had been listening in, as usual.

"No, ma'am, I've got to leave the gory details up to the minions of the law. I guess if they suspect that the guy's pacemaker failed, they'll have to dig it out and check it."

"Ugh!" she said.

"It ain't that bad, kid. No blood. All the machinery has stopped."

She came to my desk and perched on a corner. She seemed

a lot more pensive than usual. She stared out the window and embraced herself as if she felt a chill.

After a long pause, she spoke: "What do you think of Schmidt, Pat? Is he what he seems to be, a disinterested music critic?"

"He has to be interested, sweetie, or he wouldn't be a critic."

"Oh, I know that, dumbbell. Is he disinterested in the death of Theodore Blum? Or was he conning us?"

"Blum's dead. His computer crashed. He suffered a power outage. Not unusual on the Monterey Peninsula. Maybe a tree fell on him. No case."

"Where do we go from here?"

I shrugged. "Looks like this was not the terrible thing that people were spreading rumors about. We start from scratch."

"How about Bialystock?"

I had almost dismissed the little violinist from my mind. "Guess it couldn't hurt to ask him a few questions. Call the Festival headquarters. Find out where he's staying."

"Do it yourself, hawkshaw. I'm your partner, not your secretary." She flounced out.

Meekly, I opened the phone book and found the number of the Festival office. It maintains a year-round listing. I guess there's some sort of activity most of the time.

"Bach Festival, this is Lisa."

"Lisa, this is Pat Riordan. I'm a private investigator. I need to talk to one of your musicians, Mischa Bialystock. Can you tell me where to find him?"

"I'm sorry, sir, we do not give out that information."

"Look, lady, all I want is to talk to the guy. Ask him a couple of questions. You know about the death of Theodore Blum, don't you? I understand that Mr. Bialystock and Mr. Blum were old acquaintances."

"I'm sorry, sir, I can't help you." Click. Dial tone. Over and out. Egg on my face. I'm staring at the telephone in my hand. Reiko yells at me from the other side of the thin wall that separates up. "Punch line two, Pat. It's Anastasia Hawkins."

The bowlegged cellist. The lovely red-headed paramour of Carlos Vesper, who had promised to pay me to avoid any mishap to her. Couldn't have happened at a better time.

"Hi, Annie. What can I do for you?"

"I just heard that Teddy Blum is dead. Did Mischa do it?"

"Looks like nobody did it. Accidental death, I guess the coroner would call it. The guy's power system went off."

"Oh, God. I knew Teddy had that thing in his chest. What happened? Did it blow out?"

"Just stopped workin', as I get it. Simple sort of explanation. He needed the pacemaker to keep going. It stopped. He stopped."

"What a shame! Teddy could be a nasty man, but he was a terrific organizer."

A this point I had what Joyce would have called a small "epiphany." Call it a flash. Call it genius.

"Annie, do you know where I can find Mischa Bialystock?"

"Certainly, he and the other members of his quartet are in a small house at the east end of Ninth Avenue. The Festival corrals all the available rentals in town for people like us. Carlos, the dear, didn't want me bunking with anybody else, so he paid for the place we're staying in."

"Thank you, love. And give my best to the charming and debonair Carlos when he comes in."

"Oh, he's here now. Do you want to talk with him?"

"No, no. Just give him my love and tell him that I will expect prompt payment when I figure this mess out. Bye-bye."

"Wait, Pat. How well do you know Carmel?"

"Like the back of me hand, macushla. Every nook and cranny."

"Good. Then you can find the east end of Ninth Avenue."

Yeah, I said to myself after she hung up, I know it well. It's right behind my own house on Santa Fe St. There's a little piece of Ninth Avenue that runs dead on either side of Torres Street. It's a bitch to find for *auslanders*. During the last two summers I have been entertained by musicians practicing in the small house at the east end for a couple of weeks before the

Bach Festival. I've enjoyed it, honest. The house is down in what might be called a dry arroyo, about thirty feet below me. All sounds are magnified and wafted aloft. It's like sitting in the audience at the Sunset Center, only better. Better acoustics. However, in the hard rains of winter, the arroyo is anything but dry, and the water, some of which might come from the very top of Carmel Hill, swoops into this mini-valley and makes things soggy indeed.

"Reiko,"' I called, "you want to go with me to see this Bialystock? I'm leaving right now for Carmel."

"Damn right!" she said, and we hit the top of the stairs together.

"Did you lock the door, kid?"

"You bet," she said, and beat me to the car by half a block.

12

"I am Maria Genovese."

I WENT right by Ninth Avenue off Torres the first time going south. On the second pass, in the opposite direction, I slowed down and waited for Reiko to tell me where to turn. I kept telling myself that anyone could miss it. Reiko shouted: "Now!"

Just in time. I pulled a hard right and went down an impossibly narrow passage to the bottom of the hill and the end of Ninth Avenue. There were no other cars around so I pulled the nose of my badly oxidized and wounded Mercedes two-seater up against a retaining wall at the end of the street and stopped.

Reiko was out of the car in an instant. "Come on, let's go. I hear some music in there."

What she heard was the sound of a violin in the process of being tuned. Badly, I might add. Maybe Mischa was losing his hearing. Or maybe it was somebody else.

We climbed a short stairway to a small deck and Reiko banged on the door with a small fist.

"You don't have to be so rowdy, kid. We're not the cops with a warrant."

"With all that caterwauling inside, they might not hear me if I just rap politely. I better knock again."

But before she could knock the door opened a crack and a small voice said,

"Yes?" with the rising inflection that's always sounded so European to me.

Reiko spoke up: "Mr. Bialystock? My name is Masuda and this is my partner, Mr. Riordan, we . . ."

The thin metallic voice interrupted: "Mr. Bialystock is not here. He went out for a walk. He has been disturbed by the death of a friend."

Reiko persisted: "Death of a friend? Does that mean Theodore Blum? It was our understanding that Mr. Bialystock and Mr. Blum were enemies from 'way back."

There was no answer for a moment. The door opened a bit wider. The sunlight filled the doorway and we were able to see the person with whom we'd been talking.

A small woman between the ages of sixty and a hundred stood looking up at us. And you have got to be pretty damn small to look up at Reiko.

"I am Maria Genovese. I play viola with Mischa. I am also his wife. You are right that Theodore and Mischa knew each other long time. Forty years, maybe. Friends, good friends. They put on show for public. Both of them are actors. Performers. One time, long ago, they had argument before many other musicians and seemed to be near fighting. They patched it up very quickly, but both of them enjoyed the effect their shouting had on others. So they would put on shows. Forty years friends. Never real enemies."

Reiko and I were still standing on the deck. The lady had never invited us inside. "May we wait for Mischa? You don't expect him to be gone long, do you?"

"I don't know. Sometimes hours, sometimes minutes. He is a hard man to predict . . ."

"Maria!" A shout from the back of the house. "Where are you, Maria? We have got to rehearse!"

The woman's face flushed for a millisecond. But she never

lost her composure. "Oh, Mischa must have returned. But we
do have to rehearse, so, if you please, . . ."

"I'm sorry Ms. Genovese—or Mrs. Bialystock—this is extremely important. I promise you that we won't take long."
The little woman reluctantly withdrew into the house.
Lord, she was small. Couldn't have weighed more than eighty
pounds, if that. And stooped, like an advanced case of osteo-
porosis. She led us into a large room at the back of the house
into the presence of the Mischa Bialystock quartet minus one.

Mischa recognized me, I think, from our brief encounter at
the Pine Inn. But he chose not to acknowledge the fact. He
stood up, holding his violin and his bow delicately. The two
other members, second violin and cello, remained seated.

"What do you want? Can't you see we're rehearsing?"

"I'm Pat Riordan, Mischa. I'm a private investigator. My
partner, Miss Masuda, and I have been commissioned to follow up some rumors of whatcha might call foul play during
the Bach Festival. We thought the unexpected death of Mr.
Blum might be what the rumors were about. Doesn't look that
way now. They say he died of natural causes. We just want to
know if you have any ideas about some scary goings on that
might develop into bad stuff during the Festival."

Bialystock carefully laid his instrument on a coffee table
and beckoned us to follow him into the kitchen.

He bowed his head and nibbled on the second knuckle of
his right index finger.

"You were in the room, weren't you? When I arrived to see
Teddy. He had called me, too. He wanted to have us both present when he told you of certain things that might conceivably
lead to violence during the Festival."

The man looked positively spooky. Reiko dug her elbow
into my ribs. Usually it's to call my attention to something, but
I couldn't figure out what. I looked at her. She was frowning
deeply and her head was jerking almost imperceptibly toward
the door where there had appeared two more unsmiling musicians, a violin, and a cello. With Maria. The three other members of the Bialystock quartet were tuned in.

I looked at Mischa and tried to remember my first impression of him. Small, yes. Not as tiny as his wife, but small. Bald head which seemed to come to a point on top. Fringe of hair clinging over his ears and down the back of his head, rather apologetically. Deep-set eyes, large nose, receding chin. Not a beauty by any standards, but not exactly ugly, either. Lincolnesque, you might say, if Lincoln were five-foot-three.

Mischa continued to talk, even as I appraised his certain lack of beauty and stature. "Teddy and I loved to play mortal enemies. It always shook people up. We would have a terrible argument and threaten each other's lives. We played it so well. Everybody was fooled. I don't know how we got away with it over so many years. But we took pains never to be seen together in a social situation. We would meet frequently in our quarters or his for an evening of good conversation over a few glasses of brandy. We discussed many things. Both of us lost relatives in Auschwitz. Both of us were dedicated musicians. Although I . . . I have lost some of my control. Only Teddy and my wife and the other members of the quartet know why. I have Parkinson's. Do you know what that means to a violinist? It is only a matter of time until I lose control altogether."

13

"She's okay, Riordan. I can tell."

MISCHA Bialystock breathed deeply and leaned forward. "Each of has received a warning. I do not mean only my quartet. Everybody concerned with the Festival has been warned in one way or another that there will be some sort of fatal disaster during the Festival. Some have received typewritten notes. Some have had telephone calls. As far as I know—and I have talked with nearly all of the participants—there is no one who has not been alerted to this frightening problem. But we are dedicated musicians. We choose to ignore the messages as spurious. We are frightened, Mr. Riordan, but we cannot truly believe that there is someone out there who wishes to bring harm to us."

He paused and stared at the floor. "I know that there are those who believe that it is somehow the fault of poor Teddy and me. All who know us have thought us blood enemies for decades. And, as I have told you, we pretended to threaten each other in the presence of others. It was a game. A foolish game that should not have been played by grown men."

"How do we know it was a game, Mischa? You tell us this,

but Blum is dead. We really can't be sure you're telling the truth."

Another voice interrupted. "We can vouch for Mischa. Long ago he told the three of us of his little sport. We did not approve, but we love Mischa. We could not deny him a practice which he enjoyed so much."

The speaker was a tall thin man with a tall thin face. The accent was heavy, probably from Eastern Europe. As he spoke, he was twirling a cello with his left hand on the neck of the instrument. He pointed his bow at me, rather in the manner of a fencer addressing my midsection with an épée. I jumped instinctively.

"And you are?" I asked.

"Feodor Chomsky. I play cello. Mischa and I have been together for twenty-five years. Hey, Mischa, maybe it's twenty-six."

Reiko approached the fourth member of the quartet, a woman, much younger than her colleagues. "How about you? Can you back up your leader? Does all this stuff make any sense to you? What's your name?"

My partner believes in the direct approach. She fixed the second violinist with an unwavering stare, projected through her hooded eyes which she could narrow to mere slits when she wanted to.

The woman stared back. "I'm Della Fitzgerald. Mischa doesn't lie. Feodor doesn't lie. Maria always tells the truth. I may be the youngest of the crowd, but I've been with these people for five years all over the world, and I would die for any one of them. Well, maybe not die. But I would defend 'em to point of being cuffed about a little."

Reiko opened her eyes wide, grinned and turned to me

"She's okay, Riordan. I can tell."

"So, we're back to square one," I said.

I've never quite understood that expression. Is it checkers or chess? Or some other daunting game. In my dedication to the clichés of my profession, I use it again and again.

Mischa, who had been in a sort of reverie, spoke again:

"Perhaps I can be of some help after all. Do you know a music critic named Schmidt?"

Uh-oh, I thought. Schmidt again. Why is the big man's name coming up at this point?

"As a matter of fact, yes. We questioned him in his hotel room in Monterey. You think he has something to do with the rumors of disaster?"

"Yes. I am convinced that Schmidt wants the Bach Festival to fail, and that he will do almost anything to bring about that failure."

I found that a little hard to believe. Schmidt had impressed me as pretty much of a blowhard and an egocentric type, eager to find some negative aspect in any performance he undertook to criticize. But never had I got the impression that he was capable of such an elaborate plot which had not only reached all the participants in the Festival but also people like Roger Carrington.

"Thanks a lot, folks, for your cooperation. You'll probably hear from us again." I pushed Reiko toward the door. Everybody looked surprised, most of all Reiko. She followed me grimly to the Mercedes, and we zoomed out of the hollow in a hurry.

14

"I think we've got a tankful of red herrings."

As I look back over the events of that summer, nothing seems very real. Theodore Blum died in his hotel room. All the surface evidence pointed to his old friend/enemy, Mischa Bialystock. Mischa protested his innocence and pointed the finger at Evan Schmidt, the huge, black-bearded music critic. I have known critics of one sort or another in the arts to destroy the careers and reputations of artists of all sorts. But murder is carrying criticism a bit too far.

I couldn't ignore anything. Frankly, I was a bit out of my depth. I've had good luck as an investigator. And most of it can be labeled "Reiko Masuda." I must confess that I plod. I know all the routines, but there isn't an intuitive bone in my body. Oh, I have had moments of sheer inspiration. Make that really great guesswork. My charming partner is the one with the talent.

So, we were heading back to Monterey. I was concentrating on the bumper strip on the pickup in front of me that said GUNS DON'T KILL PEOPLE . . . " You know what I mean. But guns do kill people. I've seen lots of people with holes in them. Some crazy bastard with a gun. But he could have been crazy

as all hell without the gun, and the people wouldn't have died.
That seems so simple and logical to me. Why is it not to everybody? "Shit!" I said, out loud.

Reiko, who had been staring out the window on the pas-
senger side of the car, said,"Huh?"

"Did I really say that? Sorry, honey. Lost in my thoughts, I
guess."

"Me, too," she said. "And you know what I think? I think
we've got a tankful of red herrings."

"What do you mean?"

"I mean I don't think any of the people we've talked to
have had anything to do with the rumors about bad stuff at
the Bach Festival. I think there's somebody out there we
haven't met yet who's responsible."

Just as she finished that last puzzling sentence I heard a
pinging sort of sound in the car. "Damn!" I said. "I knew I
should have got premium gas."

Looking just a bit sheepish, Reiko plunged her hand into
her purse and pulled out a cellular phone. She turned away
and flipped the thing open. "Yes?" She turned back and gave
me a guilty grin. "Really?" she said to the phone. "Oh, my
God!" She listened for thirty or forty seconds, said "Thanks,"
and snapped the phone closed.

I gripped the steering wheel so tightly that the tendons in
the back of my hand elevated the liver spots to unbecoming
prominence. "When did you get that thing? Is it charged to the
office? Why didn't you tell me about it?"

"Last week. Yes. I thought you'd get mad."

"Reiko, don't you know those damn things are expensive.
And why should we even have one? We're never far from a
phone. We never get much farther away than Salinas, and
that's only eighteen miles. What the hell do we need a cell
phone for?"

"We went all the way to Florida once. That's far."

"But we were in a hotel. We had a phone. Why now?"

"You're right, hawkshaw. We don't need to call anybody.
But sometimes people need to call us. And somebody did. That

was my uncle Shiro. Schmidt's dead, Pat. Shiro just got it from one of my cousins who's a maintenance guy at the Plaza. Maid went into Schmidt's room and he was deader than . . . than . . . than a mackerel."

My jaw dropped to my breastbone. That's a figure of speech, no need to take it seriously. "Deader than a mackerel" is one, too, but I've never understood what it means. "Natural causes?" I asked.

"Nope. The guy was split from nave to chaps with a very sharp instrument."

"Nave to chaps?"

"That's from *Macbeth*. Act one, scene two. Just thought I'd throw it in. He was cut from the gut to the ribs. Like in *seppuku*."

"You got me again, kid. What's *seppuku*?"

She sniffed. "It's wrong to call it *hara- kiri*."

"You mean suicide? Schmidt cut his own belly?"

"Highly unlikely. No weapon at the scene. Just that big old body, starkers, with his insides spilled all over a fairly expensive bedspread. So what do we do now, O sainted investigator? Look for another murderer? Also like in *Macbeth*."

No, the butler is innocent, Lord Grieve-Striebling. The murderer is standing right behind you. Yes, I mean you, Lady Lilywhite. You entered the hotel room of this six-five, 280-pound man, overpowered him and disemboweled him with a hatpin. Why were these ridiculous things going through my mind? It has always been my fervent wish that a plot resolution would materialize before my very eyes like it does for all of Agatha Christie's people. Alas, I am more Wodehouse's Bertie Wooster than Christie's Hercule Poirot.

Rousing from these painful thoughts, I said: "Reiko, darlin', if you have any brilliant notions, prepare to set them forth. Or I'll give the five hundred back to Carlos."

She frowned and narrowed her eyes. "I'm thinkin'."

The cell phone made its little burbling sound again. I picked it up and flipped the little lid as I had seen Reiko do. It smelled of the inside of her purse and that unidentifiable

sweetness that always seems to hover around her. I almost forgot to say anything. "Hello, this is Riordan."

"It's Carlos, Patrick. I called your office and got a referral
to this number. Hey, how long have you had the cellular. I
think that's really neat."

"A very short time. It wasn't my idea. So what do you
want?"

"Well, goddamit, you needn't be so surly. Look, I told you
there were rumors of some nasty stuff during the Bach
Festival. Did you know there are a couple of dead bodies
already?"

"Yes. I knew. So Blum and Schmidt are dead. So are Rosen-
crantz and Guildenstern."

"That ain't the point," said Carlos, suddenly serious.
"Somebody threw a brick on our porch. I think somebody's
after Anastasia."

15

"Riordan, we've got your protégé, Vesper."

I COULD not help wondering just why some clown would throw a brick at Anastasia's house. Momentarily, I considered the pranks of the White Knights. No, I thought, Roger and his crowd would have no reason to throw a brick at somebody. They were a gentle group. No violence. Sheer stupidity to imagine that one of them would. . . .

"What the hell are you doing, Riordan?" Reiko rammed her sharp little elbow into my side. We were still in the car on the way to Monterey.

"They call it 'inner monologue,' kid. Like I'm talking to myself, but not out loud."

"Is that like when your stomach growls? You're mad about something. Or is it just gas?"

"It has nothing to do with alimentary processes. I was thinking that it just doesn't make sense that anybody involved so far in this mess should launch even such a small attack on Anastasia Hawkins. I think Vesper is suffering softening of the brain from too frequent injections of booze. Or maybe the paper guy just threw the *Herald* a little too hard against their front door, and it sounded to Carlos like a brick. I think we forget it. And if that little gadget of yours rings again, don't answer."

It's hard for me to get serious about murder. God knows it ain't any kind of entertainment. I didn't even want to imagine what Evan Schmidt's body looked like, spread out on the bed in his hotel room with his guts spilled out. Terrible stuff. I didn't like the guy, but nobody should go out like that.

It was hard to find a place to park somewhere near the office. We had to walk about five blocks. One of these days I'm going to rent a space somewhere nearby. More or less as a concession to the Parking Commission which must be getting very tired of my citations. I sort of run a charge account with them. I asked them once if they'd just take my credit card number and bill me once a month, but the lady I talked to just gave me a look of grievous pain, shook her head slowly and walked away.

As Reiko and I entered the office, I noticed a folded piece of paper which stuck to the bottom of my shoe.

"Goddam! I must've stepped in chewing gum again," I said with considerable irritation. But it wasn't gum. Some sort of sticky stuff, sure. But the paper that stuck to the shoe was a note.

I peeled the thing off my sole and unfolded it. There was a message in what looked like a feminine hand, backward-slanting so completely that it might well have been written by a left-handed person—or it was a glaring affectation. Every i was dotted with a little circle. Each little circle had a flaring tail where it was finished. The note was signed, *"A friend."*

"You gonna read it?" asked Reiko. "Or are you gonna look at it all day and not read it?"

"It says, 'You've got to look harder for the person who has sworn to ruin the Bach Festival. Two dead. Who knows what next? Get your ass in gear!' Looks like a woman's handwriting."

"Fake! 'Get your ass in gear!' That's a man's expression. No woman I know would say that."

She's right, I thought. Might be a man trying to write like a woman. Or a woman taking dictation. Or some kind of crank.

I shrugged. "Any messages?"

Reiko looked at the phone machine. "Yeah."

She punched the button and I heard the voice of my good friend Tony Balestreri of the Sheriff's Department: "Riordan, we've got your protégé, Vesper. One of our guys picked him up down on Rio Road, drunk as a skunk. You want to come get him. He says you'll bail him out."

Protégé! Tony, how could you do that to me? I had to comply, though, because Vesper, the sleazy bastard, owed me money.

What kind of a world is this? I slid off into one of my customary digressions. I am working for Carlos Vesper for money when it was the gentle Roger Carrington who approached me first with the same problem. Gutless! I've never believed in carrying a weapon, but, I thought, maybe it's a good time to pick up my trusty blackthorn walking stick. I might have time to bring it around on a bad guy before he can garotte me. Stick must be gathering dust in the old elephant's foot umbrella stand in my office.

"I'll do it, by God!"

"Talkin' to yourself again, hawkshaw? Do what?"

"Sorry. I've got to bail Carlos out of jail. And I'm sorry I've got to bail Carlos out of jail. He's a sorry sonofabitch. For that I'm not sorry."

I asked Reiko to try to get hold of Anastasia Hawkins, and I drove over to Salinas to get Carlos out of the tank.

"I've rarely seen anybody so totally out of it," said Tony Balestreri when I arrived at the jail. "He could hardly talk. Couldn't focus at all."

"Wait a minute, Tony. I had just talked to Carlos a little while before you called. He sounded a bit goofy, but not that goofy. You check his blood?"

"Yeah, that's the funny thing. Carlos was just a shade over the limit, but I've seen a lot of guys in that category who could walk straight and talk plain."

"I know I have no right to ask, but would you ask the lab to look for other stuff? Drugs, maybe."

"Okay. But they better find something. Costs money, you know."

"Thanks, Tony. I am forever in your debt."

"You're goddam right you are. And you're a few instalments behind."

I checked Vesper out of the can and dragged him to the car.

After we had been riding in silence for a while, I said,"You are really getting your buck's worth from me, buddy. Nowhere in our agreement does it say I look after you like a mama."

"Look," he said, with an expression of complete bafflement," I don't know what happened. After I talk to you—you know, about the brick—I get into my car and drive out to the Crossroads to get a belt at the Rio Grill. I'd had a few at home. I get lonesome, Pat, when Annie's rehearsing and all that music shit. I lied to you in your office. Classical music is like moose calls to me. I humor Annie. I learn what to say. But when she's away from the house I listen to jazz on the CD and get drunk. But I wasn't drunk when I left. Somehow, I found myself on the Carmel Valley Road with a sheriff's car behind me, blinkin' at me. And here I am. Hell, I've been a lot drunker and I've made it all the way to San Francisco on Highway One, even up Devil's Slide. I don't know what. . . . " He stared out the window and was silent 'til we got to Monterey.

16

"He was wearing a yarmulke?"

A DAY or so after I got Carlos back to the lovin' arms of Anastasia Hawkins in Carmel, I got an invitation to dinner from my artist friend Greg Farrell. I never refuse one of Greg's invitations. For one thing, he's a pretty good cook. For another, he's always good company. And for a third, I desperately needed a calm and rational person to talk to.

"You look stressed out, Riordan, " said Greg, as he stirred mixed greens in a very large salad bowl. "What's buggin' you, man?"

I told him about Carlos and Roger Carrington and the Bach Festival and the two dead bodies that had turned up already. I spared no gory details.

He whistled softly. "Hey, you've got a good one going there. Hang in a second while I open this can. Salad's no good without without mandarin oranges. You ever notice that? How much mandarin oranges do for a salad. Specially, if it has a tart dressing. I make my own, you know. Bottle stuff is no damn good."

I leaned back on Greg's little loveseat and sighed. The atmosphere in the little canyon just off Highway One is truly restful. I could hear the surf. The late glow of daylight saving time was tinting everything a warm gold.

Greg scooped the salad out of the mixing bowl into two smaller containers and placed one in front of me on the coffee table. "Eat," he said. "The lasagna'll be out of the oven in about ten minutes." He sat down in a wooden chair across from me and thoughtfully pursued a crescent of mandarin orange around his bowl.

"Just got back from Ojai, y'know," he said. "Went down to see an old high school friend. Hadn't seen the guy in over thirty years, but we've kept in touch, more or less. Wonderful guy. He's a Baptist minister rabbi now." He dropped the last sentence in front of me lightly, knowing it would get my attention."

"Wait a minute. He's a Baptist rabbi?"

"Yeah. Long story. When I knew him he was just Jewish, y'know. His dad was strictly Orthodox. All the dietary laws and that jazz. My friend didn't really follow the rules, except at home. We'd eat hot dogs and milk shakes together. We got in trouble together. I guess you could say he was my best friend. I didn't think of him that way back then, but I guess it's true."

"Something must have happened," I said. "You're killin' me, Greg. How'd the guy get to be . . . what he is now?" I was finding it hard to say "Baptist rabbi."

Greg shoved a large forkful of salad into his mouth and spoke as he chewed: "I hadn't seen the guy in so long, but I recognized him the minute I saw him. He was wearin' one of those dinky little caps on the back of his head and his underwear was hangin' out under his coat."

"He was wearing a yarmulke? And that undershirt. Is he Chassidic?"

"Naw, dammit, he's a Baptist. Got his own little church back in Illinois. You see he was working in Alabama, married this Alabama girl who was a Baptist. Against her parents' wishes, of course. Agreed to have the kids raised Baptist. He even went to a Baptist seminary. But he couldn't deny his father's faith. So he stayed Jewish. And became a rabbi."

"A Baptist rabbi," I said.

"Yeah."

The bell sounded on Greg's toaster oven and I never heard another word about his ecumenical-Judaic friend. We ate in silence.

"Now," said Greg, wiping his mouth and making a little tent of his napkin over his dinner plate, "what's the story? You've never accepted an invitation to dinner with me so quickly. You must need something. You and Reiko on the outs? You better treat that woman right, pal. She and I had a little thing goin' a while back but she dumped me. Can't say I blame her. I had nearly pinned that blonde waitress on the rug when Reiko walked in. But you better be good to her."

"It's this Bach Festival thing. I'm stumped, Greg. One minute I think it's all a big fake, and then somebody gets killed and I have to believe there's something to it. And, by the way, Reiko sends her best and says I would never do what you did to her. I didn't know what that meant until you told me just now."

Greg rose and began clearing the coffee table and carrying things to the sink.

"Seems to me that you're lookin' in the wrong places for the miscreant or miscreants who anticipate raising havoc at the Festival. What you're doin', Riordan, is reacting to the finger pointers. This guy tells you to look one place, that guy tells you to look another. And you go thrashing around. I think you ought to get to the center of the problem. It's a military problem, guy. Flank 'em. Flank 'em."

"What the hell do you mean?"

"Go around the edges and into the middle. Talk to everybody you can catch who has anything to do with the Bach Festival. You'll get bits and pieces, and you'll have to put 'em all together. But it takes time. How much time we got?"

"What's today?"

He glanced at a raggedy calendar over the sink. "July twelfth, looks like."

"Three days. Festival starts on the fifteenth. Seventy-two hours. How'm I gonna cover all that ground in three days?"

Greg turned from the sink. "I'll help. You and Reiko can cover some of the people. I'll mosey around and see what I can turn up. One thing, though. You'll have to fund me for all the events. I dearly love classical music, and I am a fiend for Bach."

17

"Pat, how nice to see you!"

I STOOD in his living room, wondering why I'd come out to Pebble Beach at all.He looked lot older then I remembered, but I hadn't seen him for four or five years, I guess. The white hair with the Julius Caesar haircut was the same. The lean, tanned face was . . . well, almost the same. A set of slightly curved lines that I hadn't noticed before extended down each cheek. He was stooped ever so slightly and there was an almost imperceptible stiffness in his walk.

"George Spelvin" is the name I have always used for him to protect him from his filthy rich neighbors. Not that he wasn't filthy rich himself. And George got his long before most of his affluent friends And I have always had to explain that George Spelvin is a name used in show business to plug into a cast list if the producer isn't sure who's going to play the part and the program has to go to press. It's also used to mask an actor's identity if he's doing a part that isn't really his thing, maybe as a favor to the playwright or the director.

I regard my George Spelvin as my great benefactor. It was he who insisted that I forsake San Francisco and my cheap imitation of Sam Spade to come to the Monterey Peninsula about ten years ago. I was able to persuade Reiko to come with me.

Actually George wanted me to keep an eye on his wife-of-the-moment who, he feared, was bunking occasionally with a talented and virile artist whom I shall call Greg Farrell, mainly because that's his name. Anyhow, it all ended happily. Except for a couple of ladies who got killed. One was a sweet, innocent soul and the other was an amoral witch. Sort of evened up.

All this stuff went through my mind in about five seconds as I waited for George to respond to my invitation: "Tell me all you know about the Bach Festival."

He glared. "Debbie has dragged me to that thing every goddam year since I got her out of jail. Makes her look good, she says. Makes me sick."

Debbie (a completely inappropriate name) is the lady I was hired so many years ago to keep an eye on. They got her for second degree murder. She did a year or so in one of those playground girls' camps and George got her out. I had to admire the old bastard. "She was the only woman I ever really loved, Riordan," he told me. After six or seven other wives, that is.

I rephrased my inquiry: "Are you going to the Festival this year, George?"

"Oh, shit, I guess so. Debbie likes to buy a lot of new clothes and parade around for the music lovers. I guess it's just for fun now, although I had a real suspicion that she was hot for an oboe player a couple of seasons ago. She kept telling me that a guy who could play a double-reed instrument had to be a great kisser. The embouchure, she said. The muscles of steel around the mouth. Almost as good as great buns."

I had a notion he was kidding me. "George, I'm serious. Roger Carrington approached me a week or so ago and told me that there had been threats of some sort of real nastiness to take place during the Festival. Then I heard it from a completely different and very weird source. Since that time, a conductor named Theodore Blum has died sort of mysteriously, and a music critic named Schmidt was found sort of disemboweled in his hotel room. Seems to me there is some mischief afoot, if you'll pardon the expression."

"Carrington! The old bastard doesn't know his ass from third base. Can't find it with both hands. Bats in his . . ."

"Please, George. Roger is a friend of mine. What've you got against him?"

Spelvin, who had been pacing back and forth in front of his huge fireplace, sat down wearily on one of the two excessively overstuffed and overdecorated couches in his living room. "Aw, Patrick, I really have nothing against Roger. The sonofabitch is four years older than I am and yet he always beats me at Cypress. We are engaged in ongoing verbal abuse, but I've known the man nearly forty years and love him like a brother. Like, maybe, Cain loved Abel."

I did not express what I felt at the moment. George, I knew was just past his seventy-fourth birthday which would make Roger seventy-eight. If those two old birds could still get out and bang a golf ball around, more power to 'em. I was filled with admiration.

Then Debbie came into the room. My God, I thought, she hasn't changed a bit. It had been a while since I had seen the lady. Couldn't remember just how long. But she was still as breathtaking as ever. Yeah, I'll never forget the night at my little old house at Sixth and Santa Rita when she really took my breath away. I was investigating her as a murder suspect, but, what the hell, an opportunity like that doesn't come that often.

" 'Lo, Deb," I said.

"Pat, how nice to see you!" Her teeth were white and glistening, her eyes were wide and a mysterious hazel, her hair was still blonde (with a lot of help, I guess) and her figure was . . . yes! She wore a tasteful clinging dress and the body under it was as taut as a snare drum. I got a little dizzy from the perfume of her.

"Wake up, Riordan," said George. Turning to his wife, he said: "Baby, our boy here has heard that somebody is going to blow up the Bach Festival. Does that mean that we can stay home this year?"

Two small frown lines appeared between Debbie's eyes. "It's true, then. Some of my friends have been whispering that the Festival is somehow going to be spoiled this year. But then, some of my friends are always spreading ugly rumors." She faced her husband. "No, George, we will not stay home this year. If there's any excitement to be had around this place, I want to be in on it."

I had to jump in. "Anything specific, Debbie? Like who's gonna do what to whom? Or when the bomb's gonna go off?"

"I'm sorry, Pat. All I seem to remember is that somebody is supposed to die in the middle of a performance. But I have no name."

18

"I told everybody I was a substitute French horn."

SEVERAL days passed before I heard from Greg. I was beginning to think the bastard was conning me about helping out with the approaching Bach Festival disaster. But on a bright and cheerful morning about a week before the musical orgy began, I found this neatly written note stuck precisely in the upper middle half of my office door, held with a yellow sticky thing. He must have spent some time contemplating the correct artistic balance of the effect. Greg's handwriting is also neat and precise and sometimes illegible. The note read as follows:

"Dear Pat:

I have been skimming the edges of the colony of musicians who have arrived in Carmel and vicinity and are doodling and tooting all over the place. I'm damn glad I live down the coast in a canyon. Can't understand how all you city people can put up with the noise.

"When I can get a trombone player to unpurse his lips or a mezzo to shut up, I ask questions. And bit by bit I'm getting a very confusing picture.

"Everybody knew Theodore Blum. Nobody liked him. Not one bit. Everybody knew Schmidt, the critic. Liked him even less than they liked Blum. So two guys who are gone are really forgotten with no tears. As far as I could find out, neither dead man had any sort of family. At least, nobody I talked to knew about a family. Consensus is that both were loners, mainly because they were such bastards nobody could stand to live with them.

"So. That stuff's all negative. What is intriguing, though, is that there is a general feeling among the Festival participants that somebody is going to die in the middle of a performance. These folks are superstitious, Pat. Maybe all musicians are. Or maybe just musicians who play Bach. But that isn't all they play at the Festival, so maybe I'm dead wrong.

"I'm going to have to ask you to trust my instincts, anyhow. One of the people I got some bad vibes from was this big Russian, Chomsky, who plays cello in Mischa Bialystock's quartet. Maybe it's because he looks like Rasputin, I don't know. But all the time I was talking with him, I got the feeling that he was being evasive. He seemed to be looking everywhere but at me. I got no eye contact. His eyes were wild, see, but no contact. I kept thinking about that old John Barrymore movie I saw at art school. 'Svengali' it was called. They showed it to us because of the sets and the visuals. Hell of a picture, by the way. Maybe you can find it on video.

"The notion I came away with after I had my talk with Chomsky is that he thinks that one of his quartet is the proposed victim and that Blum and Schmidt were just extra added attractions. Somebody is really out there still with murder in his heart.

"That's all for now. I'm stopping by the Art Association before I go home, but I'll keep snooping around. Hey, man, I used a great cover. I just told everybody that I was a substitute French horn."

I shook my head in deep regret. Nobody in classical music refers to that particular instrument as a "French" horn. It's just a horn, no specific nationality. Greg had probably already been detected as some kind of mole. If he had only said he was a virtuoso on the barytone, he might have passed. You don't see too many barytones in a brass section these days.

Upon reading Greg's first report, I wasn't really sure that he was going to be of any help at all in the investigation of the evil threat hanging over the Bach Festival. Unless he found a dog that did nothing in the nighttime or something equally obscure.

Reiko didn't arrive when I did. That surprised me. She is usually sitting primly at her desk staring at her computer screen by 8 A.M. She hadn't been in earlier, either. Everything was on her desk precisely as it had been the evening before. She always arranges things in a certain way: pencils here, stapler there, telephone in its proper place. Her computer doesn't take up nearly as much room as it used to. God, there were wires out of the thing leading in all directions to little boxes that buzzed or whirred or jingled. She's got a real modern up-to-date machine now that has all the other stuff inside it. Pretty soon the guys in Silicon Valley will have something you can wear on your arm. And we all thought that Dick Tracy's two-way wrist radio was far out.

The office was too quiet with Reiko not in it. No sounds at all, except my Rockports on the wooden floor. Suddenly I felt very depressed.

Then I heard a pounding on the stairs and through the hall. Reiko burst through the door and skidded into her fabulous knee-stool and picked up the phone. She favored me with a quick wave and punched out a number simultaneously.

"Shiro! Quick what's the name of our relative who works at the Plaza? The guy who told you about Evan Schmidt's death." Pause. "Lance? Not another one! Not the L.A. judge! Oh, named after him. Got a number? Thanks, uncle, I'll do you a favor some time." Pause. "Don't get sarcastic. We will pay the rent on time. And don't use that kind of language with me!"

She yelled at me on a note of what must have been triumph. "Riordan, you'll never guess what I found out!"

I was standing in the door of my own small cubicle. "You are probably dead right, kid. You have always been a puzzlement. Please enlighten me."

"They found a ceremonial knife that had slipped under the bed in Schmidt's room. He committed *seppuku*, don't you see. He was a strong believer. He was almost Japanese! Not by blood, of course. But he had spent years in Japan during the occupation. Ain't that a gas?"

19

"I don't want money, Mr. Riordan."

So, friends, if Blum died of natural causes and Schmidt committed suicide, what's going to happen next? Really, can a power failure in a pacemaker be written off as "natural causes?" And why in the world did the eminent music critic commit suicide, if he did? There was a time in my life when I could solve these problems by heading for the nearest saloon. But that was behind me now.

There hadn't been a murder or a kidnapping or an explosion to disturb the peaceful progress of the Bach Festival. The rumors and rumors of rumors persisted. Everybody looked a little guilty and a little innocent. The white-thatched Roger Carrington was probably approaching senility. Carlos Vesper was just outright nuts. The lovely auburn-haired Anastasia was child-like and, like most musicians, superstitious. I was on the verge of nervous frustration.

Damn it all! Why couldn't these people have kept their suspicions all to themselves? Why all the note-writing and the telephoning? Why didn't I just opt out and drive to Mendocino?

It was a day before the Festival was supposed to start, a

Friday. The opening night was to feature the *Brandenburg No. 3*, some Stravinsky, and, as an appropriate finale, *Hercules at the Crossroads*. I knew the *Brandenburg*, but the only image I could get of *Hercules* was a big sucker with long hair in a lion skin battling some half-naked Amazons. But it's all irrelevant. What bothered me was the fact that so many of the people had been buzzing about the catastrophe that was going to happen during the Festival and I hadn't been able to do a damn thing about it. I had even toyed with the notion that I had the right idea in the first place and that it was all a big ploy on the part of some disgruntled musician or promoter to make the Festival a financial failure. But, on the other hand, I had this sneaky notion that there was a real threat. Somebody was going to die and I couldn't do a thing to prevent it.

Greg Farrell was on the case. Reiko was on the case. I was on the case. Carlos was working his way through a case, one bottle at a time. Anastasia Hawkins was earnestly rehearsing her music. Mischa Bialystock and his group were constantly tuning their instruments. I could hear them every morning. The weather was unseasonably hot and I had to keep the bedroom windows open.

The Monterey police had just about put away Schmidt's suicide as a piece of freaky behavior. One cop's comment I heard was, "He shoulda phoned Kevorkian." His buddy said, "Yeah, I heard the guy say on '60 Minutes' that Johann Sebastian Bach was his God."

The Plaza was wondering about suing somebody for making the mess, which spoiled a lot of bedding and left a nasty stain on the carpet. Nobody yet could understand why the guy took his own life. There were a lot of disgruntled musicians around who would gladly have done it for him. Maybe. I thought there must be an explanation, but I hadn't a clue.

After examining the corpse, the proper authorities decided that Blum was the victim of an overage pacemaker. Apparently he had been advised that the thing out to be checked out every six months or so, but ignored the doctor. He'd also been told that the battery ought to be replaced after a certain length of time. He didn't pay any attention to that one, either. The little machine, about the size of an old railroad watch, its tentacles dangling into two chambers of his heart, sighed once and turned off. Blum turned off with it. No crime, just an absent-minded musician.

Reiko and I were left with an investigation that had not really gone anywhere. We were being paid to detect and prevent an anticipated debacle. We were completely in the dark.

But, as the fella once said, it's always darkest just before the dawn. Something, in the words of Micawber, would turn up. Or it had damn well better.

I was home alone. Reiko was at her aerobics class and had promised to come by later. "Law and Order" was on the TV, my favorite one-hour drama. It was about halfway through, when the cops turn the crime over to the DA, when somebody rang my doorbell. Daylight saving time drags the sun almost 'til 9:30 or 10:00. I hadn't even turned on the outside lights, something I always do down here. It's sometimes an advantage to be the last house on a dead-end street, but in Carmel at night, where there are no street lights, it's a good idea to keep on some illumination.

I opened the door to a man I'd swear I'd never seen before. He was short, slight, and nondescript. His was a face you'd never remember, one you'd gloss right over in a line-up.

"Mr. Riordan?" he asked.

"Yeah, right. What can I do for you. I gotta tell you I don't ever give money to people who come to my door. Especially people who arrive during my favorite TV show."

The man smiled. "I don't want money, Mr. Riordan. I would be very much obliged if you'd invite me in. I think I have some interesting information for you. About all the untoward events surrounding this year's Bach Festival. If you please?"

20

"I do talk too much at times."

"MY name is Gregor Samsa, Mr. Riordan. I see you smile. You are remembering Kafka's *Metamorphosis*. It is no joke, sir. My Czech immigrant grandparents came to this country in the early part of this century. My father married in the late twenties and I was born in the mid-thirties. By that time Kafka's story was already considered a masterpiece by some critics. The family name is Samsa. My mother, an Irish woman with little education but great imagination, named me Gregor. I'm not sure to this day that she ever read *Metamorphosis* or realized that the original Gregor Samsa had turned into a cockroach. But somehow she thought the name was appropriate." The small man sighed. "I am often forced into that boring explanation when I encounter one who is familiar with Kafka. And you are, are you not, Mr. Riordan?"

I shrugged. "Yeah. I'm not what you might call a 'man of letters,' but I've read a lot of books. *Metamorphosis* is a great story. Very human story. Samsa sacrifices everything for his family. When he turns into a bug they all find that they can shift for themselves. Then they forget him. Very human."

The man looked very vulnerable seated on my couch. The

84

huge, overstuffed piece of furniture made him seem tinier than he actually was. We sat in silence for half a minute or more. I thought I'd better speak first.

"What do you have to tell me, Mr. Samsa? I'd better warn you that I have been told so many things about the real or imagined troubles at the Bach Festival that I hardly know what to believe. As you probably know, there have been two deaths already. Neither seems to have had any connection to the Festival, except that both men were involved in it. Nothing spooky, nothing occult. No visitations by little green men. The guys were just dead. Cause of death established."

The small man squirmed, as if trying to find a comfortable position on the couch. "I'm aware of the deaths of Theodore Blum and Evan Schmidt. I know about the official explanations of their deaths. The police would call the cases 'closed,' would they not?"

"You bet. No mystery. No intrigue. No murder. Pretty dull stuff."

Leaning forward, Samsa said: "I'm sure that you have heard that the long so-called feud between Blum and Mischa Bialystock was a sham, perpetrated by the two men as sort of a joke. Perhaps you were told this by both men."

"Bialystock told me. Other people told me. I never really talked to Blum, except a few words on the phone when he invited me to meet him at his hotel."

The small man wrung his hands and stared at the carpet. "I am sure, Mr. Riordan, that Teddy Blum would have told you what I am about to tell you now." He stretched out his legs. I noticed that his feet did not touch to floor when he was seated. He was a very small man.

Thus he began: "I was a friend to both men. For many years. I am a pianist. Not very successful, I'm afraid. My hands are too small to begin with. And my legs are too short to reach the pedals securely. I was never good enough to ask for an especially adjusted instrument where I played. So I have spent my career as a rehearsal accompanist for singers. In that capacity I can strap blocks on the pedals, but I must simply

fake chords that I cannot reach. Singers are usually so caught up in their own voices that they never know. I never hit wrong notes, mind you. That would throw my singer off. I simply include all the right notes that my fingers will accommodate."
I'm afraid I was beginning to drift off. My eyelids were drooping, and I caught myself nodding once or twice. "Yes, Mr. Samsa, go on."
"Am I putting you to sleep, Mr. Riordan? I'm so sorry. I do talk too much at times. And I stray from the point rather often. Terribly sorry."
"Please continue, sir," I said, trying to look interested.
"The Bialystock-Blum feud was no joke." I became suddenly alert. "I was around when it began, years ago Mischa and Teddy were in love with the same woman. She was a German contralto, a lovely person. They were young men then, full of *joie de vivre*. Each would escort the lady to various functions, almost as if they were taking turns. Perhaps one or the other was anticipating a *menage à trois*. However, the relationship, whatever it was, between the two men could not continue in a friendly manner. Eventually the lady in question married a titled Englishman and left both Mischa and Teddy, as it were, standing on the dock, waving goodbye. Each blamed the other for losing the woman, although I have no idea how they expected the unusual arrangement was going to last. I know these things because I was the lady's rehearsal accompanist. I was present when she announced her engagement to Teddy and Mischa. When she left the room, Mischa slapped Teddy's face and Teddy retaliated with a sharp left hook to Mischa's jaw. They grappled with each other on the floor for a short while. Then they arose, dusted themselves off and left by different doors. I never saw them together again, except at very formal meetings when they did not speak. I am convinced that any really terrible event that is to happen during the Bach Festival will be the work of Mischa Bialystock."
I smiled at Samsa, all the while thinking, "This guy is nuts. He's a sort of police groupie. But I am not a policeman."
He was apparently finished. I stood up. "Gregor, old boy, I

am grateful for telling me all of this, but all I can think is that Blum is dead. Whether or not his misunderstanding with Bialystock is at the core of the unease about the Bach Festival, Blum is dead. Why would Mischa still want to raise hell? And why would he want to destroy any other person, or for that matter, himself? And why did you bring this stuff to me?"

His face went blank. "I was told by Anastasia Hawkins that you were hired by her friend Mr. Vesper to investigate. She told me where you were. Is my information not helpful?"

I clasped the man's hand and drew him up off the couch. Taking him firmly by the elbow, I steered him to the door.

"Thanks a lot, Mr. Samsa. Appreciate the thought. Great help. Watch yourself as you go up the street. It's darkish out now, and there aren't any streetlights here. There are potholes, however, so, above all things, don't break a leg."

21

"So, what's your tuchus telling you?"

GREG Farrell's strategy of attacking the flanks and then driving to the center was probably useful in military campaigns, but it wasn't much good for my psyche. Although I served with honor in the Army and endured the honey-pots of Korea, I am not a military person. Service in a war was something I did because I was told to. And I was a good soldier. It never occurred to me to object to anything. That's the secret of success in battle. You get a lot of guys, give 'em weapons and count on them to do what they're supposed to do.

It's a lot like a symphony orchestra, when you think about it. You give the people musical instruments, teach 'em how to read the dots on the paper, stand a guy up in front of 'em to beat time, and that's it. If the individual elements are all in some kind of agreement, the sound will be right.

It was the day of the opening concert of the Bach Festival in Carmel-by-the-Sea, California. It was indeed five o'clock in the morning, and I had not been asleep. Reiko had not chosen to join me and I lay alone, staring at the trowel marks on the ceiling. Who ever thought of that first? The skip-troweling, I mean. Conceals the tape on drywall. Ingenious. The sun is coming into my bedroom around the edges of the shades, throwing little light splashes all over in unexpected places. And I'm lying on my back wondering why I got into this crazy quilt of rumors, threats, musicians, and dead composers.

Why was I lying there comparing warfare to symphony music? If I were of a more dramatic temperament, I'd suspect that I was losing my grip on reality. But then I heard the distant sound of a bleating telephone and I knew I was in the real world.

My phone, I should tell you, is at the other end of the house from my bedroom. It's on purpose. I do not like being awakened by a phone ringing in my ear. So I keep the damn thing as far as I can from my bed. Problem is, I have to get out on a chilly morning and slog all the way to the kitchen to answer it. The advantage is, if I don't want to answer it, I just roll over.

On this particular morning, I answered it. I was already awake and my nerves were tight as banjo strings. The morning was cold and clammy (as it frequently is in July here, although some folks from the East will never believe it) and I walked barefoot and deliberate, some forty-five feet to the telephone stand.

"Yes," I said, "this better be good."

"Woke you, didn't I? That's the problem with all you round-eyes. You sleep too much," said Reiko, rather maliciously, I thought.

"Look, kid, I haven't slept all night. There was this guy who came to my door, some kind of a nut. Said his name was Gregor Samsa. Now, that's a name that was invented for a character by Franz Kafka. I think this guy was just out of his gourd. His message is that Mischa Bialystock done the deeds and that he isn't finished. I sent him away with a pat on the head."

"Whoa, buddy. Your visitor might be onto something. I've been getting little vibes here and there that the so-called act that Bialystock and Blum pulled was not an act at all. After all, what do we know? Just what Mischa told us. The others, including Schmidt, Carrington, and your lovely Anastasia, all said the feud was real but the men were pussycats. So, I've been thinkin'. . . ."

"Wait! What do you propose? It is like very early in the morning. Did you just wake up?"

She giggled. "You're not the only one losing sleep over this thing. I've been lying here since three o'clock, thinkin'. Why don't we both get up, meet for breakfast and put our heads together."

I agreed to meet her at eight o'clock at the Little Swiss Cafe in Carmel. It's the only place I know of on the Central Coast of California where you can get a decent cheese blintz. It was Saturday morning. Tourists aren't out at 8 A.M. There'd be tables in the back where Reiko and I could talk.

She was already there when I arrived, sitting in a booth, drinking black coffee. I sat down opposite her. She got up and slid in next to me. "Get your ass over, shamus," she said, and she kissed me on the cheek.

"Okay, small one, what are these vibes you're detecting that suggest that Mischa and Teddy were really carrying on a serious vendetta? Can you point to anything concrete? Or even Styrofoam? There is so much crap in the air that I get no vibes at all."

"You don't have the gift. You're still struggling with logic. All that stuff you got in law school puts you off. Look, pal, there's such a thing as being too analytical. Sometimes you gotta go by the seat of your pants." Reiko was looking terribly pleased with herself.

"So? What's your tuchus telling you? You got information that my little gray cells can't receive? Tell me quick."

By this time the blintzes had arrived, so we had to put our conversation on hiatus. They get cold if you don't dig into them right away. I needed something for my blood sugar level anyway. Reiko has a way of demanding that I be at peak mental condition when I discuss anything with her.

She looked up after she had scooped up the last forkful of blintz. "What happened to Carlos when he got tagged by the sheriff's people for speeding on the Valley Road. He told you he had a couple of drinks and then knew nothing until he saw the flashing lights in his rear-view mirror. Do you think he was telling the truth?"

She had me there. As far back as I could remember, Carlos Vesper had very seldom told me the truth—at least, the whole truth. Carlos's arrest and my bailing him out of jail were two events that I had completely erased from my memory. Didn't seem like much of anything at the time.

"Why was he driving out the Valley Road? Where was he going? Did he really know? Was he planning to meet somebody? When the cops caught him did he make up some bodacious lie?"

"'Bodacious'? Honey, Al Capp's been dead a long time. Where'd you get that word?"

"Never mind. I'm pretty damn sure Carlos was trying to pull a swift one on us, Riordan. Don't know why. It's just a feeling."

I shook my head. She gets these "feelings." She lets them lead her on and on into cloudland, sometimes. And yet, she's been right more often than she's been wrong. I really couldn't think of any reason for Carlos's escapade. Balestreri had told me that he was a shade over the line for blood alcohol, but Carlos has been known to navigate successfully with a considerable load. I can't remember his being really drunk in my presence. He is always bright and chipper in his booze, but then seizes the first opportunity to go to sleep.

That night when I drove him back from Salinas after he'd been thrown in the tank, he swore he couldn't remember much. He swore he couldn't remember what happened. But, intuitive chap that I am, I felt that Carlos was leaving something out. Something very important.

"You got that expensive little telephone with you, kid?" I asked.

"The cell phone? Sure, I always carry it. Never know when you might want to order a pizza."

"Give it to me."

She handed the little flip-phone over to me with a puzzled look. Then I had to ask her how to make a call. "You just push the buttons like any phone, wise guy. And then hit the little button marked SEND. But first pull the antenna out."

Following her instructions to the letter, I was truly amazed to find that I had got through to the Sheriff's office. In a moment I was talking to Tony Balestreri.

"What now, Riordan?" he growled.

"Bet you can't guess where I'm calling from, Tony. Go on, just take a guess."

"Don't press our friendship too hard. I'm much too busy for games. Get on with it."

"I'm callin' from the Little Swiss Café in Carmel. How about that!"

"So they got a telephone there. So what?"

"You don't get it, Tony. I'm calling from a booth. On a cellular phone. The very latest in communications equipment."

He groaned. "So why call me. If you want to practice call the 'correct time' lady."

I ignored his sarcasm. "Need an answer. Remember when Carlos Vesper was picked up for drunk on the Carmel Valley Road? I asked you to get the lab to look for other stuff in his blood besides alcohol. What did they find?"

"Nada. Nothing. Nil. I would have called you. And the lab is sending you a bill for the additional tests. Have a good day." He hung up.

22

"Is he going to be murdered?"

THE Bach Festival was finally underway. Reiko and I agreed to alternate attending the concerts. When there were two conflicting events, we'd toss for it. The Festival runs for two solid weeks plus.

"Do we have to go to the damn lectures?" said Reiko, with a very hard look in her eyes.

I hesitated. "Well, no, honey, not if you don't want to. Not if you're not interested in whatever the lecture is about. I strongly doubt that anything violent is going to occur during, say, a talk on fugues and their genesis. No. I won't go to those either."

"And how about 'Keyboard Day'? Something goin' to happen on 'Keyboard Day'?"

"I think we can skip that whole day, maybe. That eliminates a couple of Mondays."

Reiko was busy scanning the Festival program in the *Pine Cone*, Carmel's own dear weekly newspaper. "Hey, there's a 'String Master Class,' only on one of those Mondays. Do we need to go to that?"

"Bialystock won't be in it. He's no master. I think we can skip it."

The double-page spread announcing the Festival schedule was spread out on her desk. She pushed it away with an impatient gesture.

"What's gonna happen? When is it going to happen? Riordan, this is an impossible task."

"We're getting paid. We've got to cover all the bases. If nothing happens, we'll collect from Carlos and live happily ever after."

"That's another thing. Carlos's loss of memory. Going to the Rio Grill for a drink and finding himself chased by a cop car on the Carmel Valley Road. I know this guy is peculiar, but that story is so far out it's totally unbelievable."

"You don't have to believe, kid. Just go to the concerts and see if you can head off a disaster before it happens. If you can't, dial 911."

I heard a footstep very near. When I looked up, Greg Farrell was standing two feet away from me with a wide grin on his face.

"God, you two concentrate like nobody's business. I've been here for a whole minute and you didn't even know it."

"You are Chingachgook, last of Mohicans, you sneaky bastard. Why didn't you knock?"

"Gee, I thought you'd be glad to see me. I bring news. Exciting news. I know exactly when the awful event is going to transpire at the Festival."

I looked at Reiko and she looked at me. We slowly shook our heads.

"And I thought Carlos Vesper was the only real nut involved in this business," said Reiko.

"No, really," said Greg. "I have accurate information that a musician of the stringed instrument variety is going to die onstage in the middle of a number."

"What kind of string," said Reiko, acidly. "Pianos have strings, harpsichords have strings, as well as violins, violas, cellos, bass fiddles, and harps. The category includes about two-thirds of the participants. Did you get a name, cowboy?"

Greg looked hurt. "What do you expect? The one thing that everybody I talked to seemed to know was that some kind of musician who played a stringed instrument was going to die during a performance."

I came to life. "Is he going to be murdered? Or maybe is she going to be murdered? And by what method? Eliminate defenestration. Will it involve a knife or a gun? They're not playing the *1812 Overture,* Greg, they never play the *1812 Overture,* like where the cannons can mask a gunshot."

"You think I'm crazy, too, Pat. Look, I said I'd attack this thing from the flanks and drive to the center. Nobody has confessed planning a crime. But everybody seems to know something about what's going to happen. I don't know all the details, but somebody is going to die. Onstage. During a concert."

I could not imagine how Greg could be so completely convinced. In his mind, I guess, the fact that so many people told the same story was enough.

"Thanks, pal. I appreciate all your work. Now go back to your studio and paint. Maybe you can come up with an impression of a macabre murder occurring in the theater at the Sunset Center. Rivulets of blood running up the aisles, accompanied by violins bursting into flames. Go rest, Greg."

I'd like to say I didn't hurt his feelings. I'd like to say he wasn't indignant. But I've never seen him with such a bleak look on his face. He turned on the heel of one boot and clomped out of the office.

"You encouraged him," said Reiko. "You let him go around pretending to be a horn player. It's all your fault."

I did feel a little embarrassed. Greg is possibly my best friend in the world. Male, that is. And I brushed him off.

I pressed my hands against my temples. "Maybe he's right. Maybe he got some information along the line that is accurate. But who's going to do what to whom and when?"

Reiko sighed. "We will have to go to all those damn concerts, won't we?"

I became lost in my thoughts. I can get lost almost anywhere. The most significant piece of information that was still missing was the strange tale of Carlos Vesper's arrest on the Carmel Valley Road.

"Come on, kid. We're going out to talk to Carlos again."

23

"What now, genius?" asked Reiko.

THE house on Lincoln Street was dark when we arrived. There were no outside lights, and it appeared that no light was left burning inside. When this happens after dark in the unlighted streets of Carmel, the darkness is all-consuming. Seldom is there a moon in the summertime. The coastal fog sweeps in during the evening and settles overhead. It may hang around for a day or a week. At night it effectively blots out any light from the heavens.

"What would Sherlock Holmes have done?" hissed Reiko.

"In London they have lights. Not very good lights, but lights anyhow. It is never as black as it is in this town. Holmes might have tripped over a dead body, but he wouldn't have walked into a wall."

We felt our way across the lot on the crooked path of flat stones to the bottom of the stairs, which I discovered by severely bruising my right shin on the bottom step. Holding tightly to the unsteady bannister I pulled myself up the narrow staircase to the tiny stoop. Reiko followed, hanging onto my belt.

Standing before the door of the little house, we couldn't even see each other's faces.

"What now, genius?" asked Reiko.

"Knock on the door, I guess. You got something better?"

"Try the knob. Save a lot of time and trouble."

I did, and the door opened into another mess of total blackness. "Where's the light switch? " I asked.

"How should I know? I've never been here before. You feel over there and I'll feel over here. Should be somewhere near the door."

In a few seconds the lights went on with a little cry of triumph from Reiko. "I knew it. Shoulder high on the right hand wall. Gee, what an ugly room!"

The room was ugly, I guess. I hadn't noticed before, possibly because I was so taken with Anastasia's beauty. Like a lot of Carmel short-term furnished rentals, it had a couple of mismatched chairs and a couch that had seen better days. There was a coffee table that bore evidence of many cups of coffee and countless other beverages. Three lamps that produced maybe 180 watts of light. An empty bookcase. The remains of yesterday's newspaper. A color TV with no remote. A fireplace that hadn't been cleaned, maybe ever.

Beyond the living room we could see a short hall probably leading into the bedroom. I led the way as we plunged once again into darkness out of reach of the meager living room illumination. "Ha!" said Reiko, banging her hand against the wall. An overhead light, a single bulb came on. We passed a closet-sized bathroom and arrived almost immediately into another dark space that had to be the bedroom. By this time we had explored the whole house. If this was the deluxe space that Carlos was paying for, it wasn't much luxe.

The bedroom revealed nothing. No Carlos, no Anastasia. Well, the cellist was probably rehearsing, I thought. God knows where Carlos is. There was no back way out. No entry or exit except the front door that we had opened innocently, you understand, out of curiosity.

"Let's just go in and sit down. Maybe somebody will show up. I saw some M&Ms in a dish on the coffee table." Reiko is always practical.

We sat and stared at the cold fireplace, eating M&Ms. Reiko tried the TV once, but couldn't find the power switch. "They do that on purpose, I bet. So you won't turn it on and use the electricity. Cheap, Riordan, cheap."

I'm not sure just how long we were sitting there when we heard a car pull into the driveway. Well, it really wasn't a driveway, just a kind of notch off the street. There are no sidewalks in Carmel when you get out of the business district. Even the smallest houses have some sort of access for one automobile, maybe just long enough and just wide enough for a compact.

We heard voices, male voices, coming into the yard and footsteps, heavy footsteps coming up the steps.

"Hello, anybody home?" one voice asked.

"We're here, but we're just visitors," I called.

"Riordan? Pat, is that you?"

The second voice was very familiar. Tony Balestreri had what we used to call in San Francisco a "Mission Accent." The Mission District was mostly Italian and Irish for a long time. And the inhabitants talked like their forbears who had come from New York and New Jersey.

"Tony? What the hell are you doing in Carmel?" I had got up and stood in the doorway. "You're out of your jurisdiction."

"Just barely, kid. I'm investigating a crime that occurred outside the city limits, on the Point. Badly beaten female corpse. Apparently white, approximately twenty-five to thirty, five-three, maybe 120 pounds."

"Was she a redhead, Tony?" I had this terrible feeling that it must be Anastasia.

"Who can tell?" he said. "They all color their hair, don't they?"

"I sure don't!" said Reiko. "You're some kind of pig, Balestreri."

"Look, kid, no offense. It's just that we got this report on the phone that the guy we should be lookin' for has been stayin' in this house."

"What do you mean, 'report on the phone'? Anonymous?"
I asked.

"Yeah, when we got the call on the body. Tried to get the
caller's name, but he hung up."

"Where's the body?"

"Still in the bag. In the van."

"Is the van still here? Can I take a look?"

"Sure, come on downstairs."

I followed Balestreri out to the street. His police car was in
the little parking area, and the van with its bored and drowsy
driver was parked in the street. The driver got out and opened
the double doors at the rear of the van. A fairly bright dome
light came on like the light in your refrigerator. The driver
unzipped enough of the body bag to reveal the woman's face.

"It's not Anastasia," I said, with a loud sigh of relief.

The woman had been badly beaten, at least around the
head. The face was beaten to hamburger. But it wasn't
Anastasia. The hair wasn't right.

"Then who the hell is it?" asked Reiko.

24

"Sorry, honey, too many corpses."

DESPITE the fact that I have had to look at many dead bodies in my time, I still get a terrible feeling in the pit of my stomach. Some dead bodies—Theodore Blum, for instance— just look like people whose vital signs have signed off. I mean, Blum had his eyes open. His color had not yet change into the waxy pallor that dead people assume after the passage of some time. But it still made me sick to look at him.

In Korea I saw a lot of dead bodies and pieces of dead bodies that had come about as the result of chunks of metal travelling at a very high speed. Heads were sometimes separated from torsos. Limbs were shredded or missing. They said I'd get used to it, but I never did. I just waited for the sun to rise. When it did, I knew I had some more daylight hours left. Then there would be another day of noise and fear and flying chunks of metal.

It's been a long time, and I don't have nightmares anymore. But looking at the brutalized face and head of a reasonably young woman in a body bag got to me. I got out of the van and walked aimlessly up the block.

Reiko caught up with me, puffing. "Where the hell do you

think you're going, Riordan? That woman in the bag. We've got to find out who she is. Your old buddy Vesper is somehow connected to her. Maybe he killed her. Didn't she look like anybody you'd seen before? Carlos couldn't know many people on the Peninsula. He's been gone for a couple of years."

She grabbed my elbow and I stopped, still in sort of a haze from the rush of memories. "Sorry, honey. Too many corpses. I forget sometimes that we live in an unsteady world." I breathed a couple of lungfuls of the fresh night air and we walked back to my car.

"It's very hard to tell what a human being looked like after it has been bashed like that one. I knew it wasn't Anastasia by her hair. Anastasia is a red-head. This woman's hair is very dark. But that's all. The face was so badly smashed I couldn't tell anything else. It was almost as if she was beaten that badly to keep her from being identified. There might have been something vaguely familiar about her, but that's just a gut feeling. Nothing I can describe. Nothing I even want to talk about."

"Let's go home, Pat. Your place. I think you've done enough for one day. And so have I. I didn't get the same feeling, looking at that dead woman. I haven't had the experiences you've had. Maybe I'm just too tough for my own good. Let's go home."

Reiko drove us up the hill to my house after I had promised Balestreri that I'd let him know if I turned up anything. "You better, buddy," he said. "There's an awful lot goin' on around here for this time of year. I'd like to put an end to it. Keep in touch."

We got home. It's your home, I keep telling Reiko. Your Japanese garden, your Japanese gate, whatever you want. Your mama would approve, although I know she still mistrusts me.

I felt relieved as we went through the door. The familiarity of the place was a comfort to me. The pain in my gut began to subside.

"I'll whip up some decaf," said Reiko. "It's too late to drink real coffee. I don't think caffeine keeps me awake. Maybe you, though."

As she busied herself in the kitchen, I walked out onto the back deck and looked down at the house where Bialystock and company were staying. The lights appeared to be on in every room in the house and on the porch. The bright carport light was illuminating the street. But there was no car parked in it.

I didn't hear any sounds from the house. No music, no tuning of strings. It was dead silent. Dead, as in dead body. I felt a little chill. If those people had gone to bed, why were all the lights on? If they hadn't gone to bed, why couldn't I hear anything? The way the little canyon works, you can hear the slightest sound from where I am on the slope above. It's embarrassing sometimes when I can hear conversations conducted in normal tones below me, even when I don't want to hear them. But I can't keep the doors and windows closed all the time.

"Here, slugger, have a cup of decaf." I took it from Reiko's hand. "Hot enough for you?" she asked.

"Sure."

"What are you looking at?"

"House down there. Nothing stirring. I'm trying to figure out why. Probably nothing wrong. Probably they're all sitting around reading or thinking or playing cards. That doesn't seem right, though. I never was in a card game where nobody made any noise. Aw, shit. I need a good night's sleep."

But just as I took Reiko's hand and turned to go back into the house, a car made a skidding turn into Ninth off Torres, came barreling down to the dead end and pulled into the carport below. The car doors were open even before the vehicle came to a full stop. Three shadowy figures slammed doors and rushed into the house. There was a babble of excited voices, then silence. Then the lights in the house went out, one by one.

25

"And I think you're a pig, sometimes."

IT was the following Tuesday. Reiko and I were scheduled to attend a performance of Bialystock's string quartet playing something or other that I had never heard of. But there wasn't much on the schedule of the entire Festival that I had ever heard of. Classical music, as I have said, is not my forte. I like a lot of it, but I can't really remember the names of any of the pieces. Except maybe Beethoven's stuff. His symphonies run one through nine, and I can remember numbers. I can even hum the last part of the ninth.

I never told Reiko that I had taken clarinet lessons in elementary school. Well, she had never told me about her violin, either. I mulled over the possibility of confessing my own rude musical beginnings to her, but I decided against it. I never learned to read music. When I was in the band or orchestra, I'd listen to what the guy in the next chair was playing and, second time around, I could play it just as well as he did. The spots on the staffs on the music sheets didn't mean a thing to me. Later I got pretty good at improvisation and could play jazz well enough.

But the thought of sitting through a couple of hours of a

string quartet dismayed me. Reiko refused to go without me. It was actually her turn, but she wouldn't budge.

"I gotta suffer, so you gotta suffer, "she said. "We're partners, right? We share and share alike, right? So we go to this thing together."

So we found ourselves in the crowd moving slowly into the auditorium at Sunset Center on a Tuesday evening in July. The sun was still shining, low in the west, and breeze off the ocean was just right. It was a night for doing just about anything other than sitting through the performance of a string quartet.

The capacity crowd had moved into the auditorium with a loud murmuring of unintelligible conversation. It was just human noise, know what I mean? A pretty good volume of sound, but no words. Reiko and I found our seats and settled into them. I looked around at the audience.

"I hope everybody doesn't have to go to the john at intermission. The line for the ladies' room usually stretches out to the street. I never understood why women had to have stalls to pee. Why can't they just straddle a urinal . . ."

"Shut up, Riordan! People are listening to you. They don't know you like I do. And I think you're a pig, sometimes." Reiko's elbow seemed to get sharper every time she jabbed it in my ribs.

The lights began to go down in the house. The four participants in the concert filed onto the stage, carrying their instruments. Mischa Bialystock remained down center while his cohorts stood behind them at their chairs. He accepted the polite applause with grace and smiled. It was a practiced gesture. A smile to the left, a smile to the right, a slight bow, a wave to his group, smiles and small nods from them, they all sit down.

The music began. It was strange and wonderful and soporific. About sixteen bars into the first selection I began to drowse. Reiko gave me the elbow again. I resigned myself to staying awake. I couldn't take much more of that elbow.

For the first half-hour, I sat, less than transfixed. The music sounded all right to me. Bialystock was playing and I couldn't hear any sour notes. He seemed to be in command. He gave the cues and the others seemed to pick them up, glancing briefly at the first violin.

At the end of their first offering, Mischa stood up to accept the applause of the crowd, which impressed me as a shade more than polite but less than enthusiastic. He directed his comrades to rise and they did. They all sat down together and started to play again.

We didn't have a program. It wouldn't have meant much to either of us anyhow. The same routine was repeated again and again through the evening. There was a twenty minute intermission during which we strolled into the lobby and watched the women, some of 'em pretty desperate, waiting in line at the ladies' rest room. Twenty minutes would not be enough. Some of the women wouldn't make it until 'way after the second half of the concert started.

What happens is, I guess, that a lot of the folks at the concerts go to little parties beforehand and sip martinis and manhattans and that stuff. It percolates through the system, timed to hit during the concert. They suffer. I've seen strong men shove others out of the way to get to the urinal at events like this one.

I think I might have snoozed with my eyes open for a time during the second half of the program. Suddenly I was aware of Reiko's elbow again and a roar of appreciative applause from the audience. It was over.

The lights went up in the auditorium before the musicians left the stage. Bialystock left first, then his wife, Maria, then Chomsky, the cellist, and last, the second violin whatsername, Della Fitzgerald. I looked again. It wasn't Della. It was somebody else. A totally different somebody. About the same height, weight and age of Della Fitzgerald.

"Reiko," I whispered. "That isn't the same violinist we met the other night."

She whispered back: "I wondered when you'd notice that. I knew it as soon as they came on the stage. But you kept dozing off. We'll have to go see the Bialystock string quartet. Tonight!"

26

"Knock, dammit, knock."

WE left the Sunset Center Auditorium before the last number of the evening. The evening had turned chilly with the arrival of the customary high fog. A breeze stirred the live oaks and swayed the Monterey pines.

"So what do we do now, O all-seeing one?" asked Reiko.

"Be damned if I know. Do those people go home right after their performance? Or do they hang around to hear the other works on the program?"

"Tell you what. Let's just go up to your place and keep watch. Won't turn on the lights or anything. Just watch. See when the quartet comes home. If it comes home. Maybe it'll come home with four people. Maybe it'll come home with three. Then where's the fourth?"

We found my car on Eighth Avenue and drove the few blocks up to my place on Santa Fe. I'd left the front lights on as usual, so we didn't have any trouble with negotiating the steps and getting in the front door. I don't know why we were so quiet. The night was dead black all around us save for a light or two, left on like mine to give the resident something to aim at when he arrived home.

We took up positions in the room I sometimes use as an office. Well, it's got a desk in it and a telephone. That makes it an office, doesn't it? Neither of us tried to make conversation. We just stood dumbly staring out the window down into the little canyon, waiting for . . . well, waiting for I don't know what.

In a little while headlights appeared at the top of the hill opposite us, making the swing into Ninth Avenue and down the hill. The car moved very slowly and turned into the carport of the house directly below us. The doors opened and three people got out. Soundlessly, they mounted the steps to the small deck and disappeared through the front door. Lights began to come on in the house from front to rear. At least three quarters of the Bialystock String Quartet had arrived.

"What now?" whispered Reiko. "Do we go down there. Do we make like we've just dropped in for a nice glass of tea. What?"

"We just walk down calmly, knock at the door and see what we find. Or whom we find."

It is possible to get down to the dead end of Ninth Avenue from the dead end of Santa Fe Street by stumbling through a patch of city-owned trees on an ill-defined path, It is difficult in broad daylight. It is well nigh impossible in the dark of night. I rummaged through what I call my junk drawer to find my small flashlight so that we would have a better chance of avoiding serious injury on our way down the hill.

Reiko held my hand as I bravely led us into the woods. The title number from Sondheim's *Into the Woods* kept running through my mind. Da de de dump, da dump da dump.

"You're breakin' my hand," whispered Reiko through her teeth. "Leggo, Riordan. I can make it," she said, at which moment she slid on her backside.

It was fortunate she could not see my look of scorn as I picked her up.

We reached the level of Ninth Avenue. Most of the lights in the house were on now, including the very bright light in the carport. There was no longer any need for my puny flashlight, but I forgot to turn it off.

I stood before the front door not sure for a moment exactly what I wanted to do.

"Knock, dammit, knock," hissed Reiko. "And turn off the damn flashlight."

I knocked. There was movement inside. I heard footsteps approaching the door. There was some conversation in the background which I couldn't understand before the door was opened just a crack and Maria Genovese peeked out, just as she had the first time we visited. This time she recognized me.

"It is Mr. Riordan, no? Why do you come here at this time of night? We have told you all we know. Please, we are very tired. Go away, please."

"Sorry, ma'am, but there's something we've got to ask you. We were at your performance tonight, and I noticed. . . . ah . . . that you had a different second violinist. It wasn't Miss Fitzgerald. Is she ill?"

There was an uncertain pause. "Della was called away. Suddenly. Somebody telephoned last night. A relative, I believe. Della left this morning. We were fortunate to be able to get a substitute so quickly. But there are many violinists here, and they are all very competent. The woman we asked to play with us was familiar with the composition. No one could have known the difference."

"Any idea where Miss Fitzgerald went? Know where her family lives? Did she drive, did she fly, did she go by bus?"

A sharp voice came from inside. "Let them in, Maria. We have nothing to hide."

The woman stepped back and opened the door. Mischa Bialystock was standing in the middle of the room, looking somehow larger and more formidable than he had looked before. It was hard for me to connect the Mischa who stood before me now with the Mischa who had collapsed in the doorway of Teddy Blum's hotel room.

Bialystock smiled. "It is very simple. As Maria has told you, poor Della received bad news from her family. It was only right that she should go home. I do not know where her family is, nor do I care. She joined us in New York. She was possibly the best prospect out of Juillard. I listened to her play. I did not ask her pedigree."

The man was very cool. I couldn't help thinking that he had presented several different images to me. Which one is real?

"Well, thanks, Mr. Bialystock. Sorry to have disturbed you, But you see, a young woman's body, beaten beyond recognition has been found not far from here, and we noticed that Miss Fitzgerald wasn't with you tonight, so we thought that maybe. . . ."

"Ridiculous!" said the small bald man, bristling his nastiest bristle. I swear he shook for a moment at such a high rate of speed that he seemed to be blurred. An ultra high frequency shake.

I backed into Reiko and stepped on her foot. She gave forth a Japanese hiss of great rage, but said nothing.

"Sorry to have bothered you, Mischa. Get a good night's sleep. Thanks a lot. Extend my sympathy to Della if you hear from her. Seemed like such a nice girl. . . ."

"Come on, Riordan," shouted Reiko in my ear. "We've overstayed our welcome.

But, of course, there had been no welcome.

27

"This is Meredith. Speak."

WE trudged wearily up the hill, stumbling in the dark.

"Where's your damn flashlight now, Riordan?" Reiko sounded fierce.

"Battery's dead," I answered, truthfully. It had been months, I guess, since I last used the small flashlight. Last time the power went off. December, when a very tall pine snapped off and took out a section of my back deck. I looked out that time and could only see large branches of pine and cones scattered all over the deck outside my bedroom. I can remember now the terrible sinking feeling I had. The wind was still howling outside and I huddled in the living room during the blackout which ensued, waiting for the rest of the tree to fall. It didn't.

"What are you thinking about?" asked Reiko. "I'll bet it's that dumb storm last winter. You were lucky, hotshot. Three feet to the north and that big ol' hunk of tree could have smashed you in bed. I'm damn glad I wasn't with you."

"You would have been terrified, kid. I took the whole thing in stride. Like a man."

"Bullshit," she said, softly.

When we got within range of my outdoor lights, we walked

a little faster and a whole lot straighter. My living room
seemed brighter and more inviting than ever before. We sat
down wearily on the couch.

"Want me to start a fire?" I asked.

"Too much trouble," she said. "Besides that flue hasn't ever
worked properly. Place stinks like smoke every time you burn
a teeny piece of wood in it."

I leaned back and closed my eyes. "Reiko, I've been thinking about Evan Schmidt."

"What! Schmidt's out of it. Way out of it. Spilled his guts,
you might say. Literally. Why Schmidt?"

"We've taken it for granted that the guy was immersed in
Japanese tradition and committed what you call *seppuku*.
That's the thing where a guy stabs himself in the gut and pulls
the knife up to the breastbone. Why would anybody do that?"

"Irredeemable disgrace. Loss of face. Failure to bow in the
presence of the Emperor. Who knows?"

"What do you suppose could have prompted a guy with an
ego the size of Detroit to commit suicide? Hard to believe."

Reiko frowned. She got up and walked toward the fireplace
and stood with her back to what would have been a cheery fire
if she hadn't vetoed the idea.

"You started something, Riordan. I just eliminated Schmidt
from this whole affair when he killed himself. Didn't really
think about why he did it."

Both of us were silent for some minutes. I stared at the ceiling, still awed by the trowel marks in the mud that wall guys
use to cover the taping.

"Let's find out more about Schmidt. And how he got so
goddam Japanese."

Needless to say, Reiko spent the night at my place. She does
keep a few things in one drawer of my dresser and about a
third of my closet. Actually, she doesn't need much. Well, a
toothbrush, maybe.

Anyhow, we went to the office together the next morning
and began to check out ways to get more dope on Schmidt.

The Plaza told us that the man had not given them a specific address. Just signed the register, "Evan Schmidt, San Francisco." The body, they informed us had been taken first by the paramedics to Community Hospital of the Monterey Peninsula, whose acronym, CHOMP, always makes me a little uncomfortable. The hospital told Reiko that the body had not been claimed, but had been sent to a local funeral parlor for safekeeping and, I guess, refrigeration.

The funeral home reported that nobody had claimed the body and if we were friends there were some mounting charges. I politely declined the honor and asked them please to let us know if anybody showed up or called.

"Didn't the sonofabitch have any friends?" asked Reiko. "Surely there is a person in this world who was close enough to this guy to want to see him disposed of in a dignified manner."

Only then did I remember that my own inquiries about Schmidt had met a dead end when I couldn't reach the party I wanted to talk to at the *Herald*. I called her.

"This is Meredith. Speak."

"Merry, this is Pat Riordan. Need a favor."

"Ain't it always the case. What's up, Patrick? Be quick. I'm doing a very long piece on the Bach Festival. Music's my beat, you know."

"That's why I called. This'll be quick. You know . . . knew Evan Schmidt."

"Yes, and I don't miss him one bit, if that's what you mean."

"Not exactly. Schmidt is supposed to have killed himself in a very special way."

"Yeah, I heard. *Hara kiri.* Belly cutting. Just like the guy. Had to make a big production of it."

"That's just it, Merry. What do you know about Schmidt's background that would make him go through such a nasty, bloody ceremony?"

She thought a moment. "He did go to Japan every year. But most of the musicians that are here for the Bach Festival go all over the place, including the Far East. There's never been any talk about Schmidt taking those old Japanese traditions seriously. Seems like a big joke to me."

I wasn't satisfied. "Forget about the method. Can you think of any reason for Schmidt's committing suicide."

"That's a lot easier. Inoperable malignant brain tumor. Didn't you know that?"

Well, hell no, I didn't know that. Nobody had said that. Why had nobody said that? "Common knowledge?" I asked.

"Not really. I asked him once why he was so damn nasty in his criticisms. He told me he just had to be. It was the one thing that gave him pleasure. That was when he told me about the tumor. My theory is that when he heard about Teddy Blum's death, he just went 'round the bend. Had one of his excruciating headaches, went to one of those Oriental curio stores in Monterey and bought a big knife."

28

Nothing in the high-tech world is safe, I guess.

MAYBE, just maybe I had figured things all wrong. Honest, I don't do that very often. Most of the time I take a strictly logical approach to a problem, add in Reiko's intuition, divide by two and add anything else I may pick up and, voila, solve the crime. If it is a crime. Or if I can't remember how many shirts I sent to the laundry. Or I can't remember whether or not I paid the Pacific Gas & Electric company's latest bill. Or if I had an appointment for any time on any given day.

Reiko had left the office for some mysterious reason. She rarely tells me where she's going or what she's going to do. I was sitting in my swivel chair, marveling at a new set of noises it made, wondering whether it was time to trade it in. When I closed my eyes, I got a quick vision of the lump of Theodore Blum's body on the bed in that hotel room. That's what it was. A lump.

But why a lump? Blum was lying on his stomach, head turned to one side, eyes open, mouth open, a tiny drop of drool at the corner of his mouth. But he was a lump when I first caught sight of him. Why?

I stopped swiveling and sat up straight. He was covered with a quilted bedspread. Not just up to his neck, but covered. All over.

Was he taking a nap? Ridiculous. He was expecting me. He had called me and invited me to meet him in his hotel room. Had he gone into some sort of convulsion and pulled the spread over his head before he died? Highly unlikely, I thought. A guy who is dying because his pacemaker has failed would just pass out. What better way to go? No pain, no strain. Just zip, nada, nothing. The joke is over.

It was the opinion of the medical people that Blum had died because of his own damn ignorance. He had been told to have the pacemaker checked every six months. He had been told that the battery was good for a limited time. He had paid no attention to the advice of several cardiologists. He knew he was dependent on the little round thing stuck under the skin in his chest, but he chose to forget, ignore, challenge . . . I don't know what. And he died.

Sometimes a great notion—Kesey wrote a book with that title, didn't he?—will take you from behind. Truthfully, I am not frequently ambushed by great notions. But it occurred to me during this quiet reverie that it might have been possible for a person or persons unknown, somebody who knew about Blum's pacemaker, and, possibly, knew about his irresponsibility about having the thing checked, could have used some artificial means to short the damn thing. It runs on a battery, right? Battery produces electricity, right? The human body is electrical. Where the hell did I learn that? There is something called the sino-atrial node, a little projection inside the heart that produces the regular impulses that make the heart beat in the proper rhythm.

My God, I could not believe all this stuff was coming back to me from a course in human biology I took about forty years ago.

Why not? Couldn't there be some means of interfering with a pacemaker from the outside to make it stop? Or make it speed up?

I called a cardiologist that I knew slightly at Community Hospital. When I put the question to him, he was just a touch evasive. "Couldn't happen. These things are foolproof now. Used to be some problems with microwaves, but not any more. Pacemakers are getting better all the time. Soon there'll be one the size of a nickel that'll last probably forever."

I pressed him. "How about one that's been in use for a long period of time by a guy who was convinced he couldn't die and didn't go regularly for checks."

"Really, no. At least I don't think so. Any guy who's dependent on a pacemaker would make sure to follow doctor's orders. Nobody would be arrogant enough to think he couldn't die."

I continued: "How about this? The guy has a heart problem somewhere in Europe. He needs the pacemaker. Some guy in France or Italy installs it. Gives him the warning speech. Tells him to get in touch with his doctor as soon as he gets back to the States. He forgets what he's been told. He goes right on doing whatever he's always been doing."

Momentary silence from the other end. Finally: "It's a crapshoot. Depends on how old the guy's device is. When it was implanted. The state of the leads that go into the heart. I don't know. Recently I've heard that using a cellular phone can adversely affect a pacemaker. I tell all my patients to use their right ears on 'em."

"Thanks, doctor. You've been very helpful. If I ever have a heart attack, I'll call you."

He laughed. "If you ever have a heart attack, you've got a good chance of dying. Initial attacks are the killers. If you have chest pains, call me. If you have a persistent pain in your left arm, call me. Some chest pains, angina pectoris, are controllable medically. But don't let 'em get too far."

I thanked him again and took my pulse. The one thing that I have feared in my life, aside from a bunch of North Koreans and Red Chinese, is a heart attack. There's no history in my family that I know of. But I've lost a few close friends. And I ain't as young as I used to be.

I filed the information from the doctor in the back of my mind, including what he said about cellular phones. Reiko had bought that cell phone, dammit. Cell phones and cordless phones had been suspected of being involved in creating brain tumors or something because the radio frequencies were emitted so close to one's head. That turned out to be so much bullshit. I think.

Nothing in this high-tech world is safe, I guess. We keep inventing things that turn out to be carcinogenic, things that melt the enamel off your teeth, things for the betterment of mankind that somehow create misery for mankind. Things that are supposed to be for the common good that are really adaptable to killing people by the thousands. No cure for cancer, no cure for AIDS. Happy pills for unhappy people.

I was really getting depressed. In the old days I would have gone out and got drunk. Now I had this terrible craving for a banana split.

Reiko appeared in the doorway and I managed to smile. "Where you been, honey? I missed you."

She cocked her head and raised an eyebrow. "Missed me? Whaddaya mean, missed me? You never say anything like that. Okay, what did you do, Riordan? You been goofin' off? You had a call girl in here and you're afraid you left stains on the floor."

I rose from my chair, went slowly around my desk and walked up to her. I took her face in my hands and very quietly kissed her for maybe a little less than a minute.

She pulled back and looked at me with an expression of awe. "What was that all about? You win the lottery? I know, you've been takin' a lot of those male hormone things you keep telling me about. Whoa back, big guy! This is a place of business." And then she threw her arms around my neck and kissed me back.

She stepped back and pushed me away, brushing off her skirt and straightening her hair. "Business, please. Save the other stuff for a more appropriate venue. I have some pretty fair news for you."

"What do you mean, fair? Am I gonna like this news? Is it stuff that I really want to hear? Did one of your relatives leave you a lot of money?"

"The body of the girl that they found has been identified. Don't ask me just how, because I don't know yet. It was the second fiddle, Pat. It was Della Fitzgerald. Of the Bialystock string quartet."

29

"I . . . I've got a . . . sort of confession."

IT seems that the medical examiner had tried all sorts of various ways to identify the body of Della Fitzgerald. Fingerprints couldn't be matched. Blood type was common. DNA wouldn't work if you had nothing else.

At last, a woman in charge of the dead girl's personal effects, which consisted of her clothes and her shoes was casually examining a rather expensive sweater she was wearing when the body was found and found a cleaner's mark on the label: "D. Fitz."

This was no tribute to forensic science. This was pure luck. The body was the right size and weight for Della, all right. But the face was so battered that her own mother wouldn't have recognized her. She had been beaten with a heavy blunt instrument and her face had been deliberately smashed, I'm sure, to prevent identification. The killer obviously didn't know about laundry marks or he just didn't think about 'em.

The big question was: Why Della Fitzgerald? Reiko and I had met her once with the other members of Bialystock's string quartet. I really couldn't remember much about her. She was a lot younger than the other three. I think what went through my mind (and I'm a little ashamed of this) was, "What's this young Irish-American girl doing with these old European musicians?"

I could not imagine what sort of connection to this crazy plot the young violinist had. My quick impression of her had been that she seemed so innocent, so happy to be accepted by established musicians. And young. I thought of Anastasia Hawkins, the still-youthful cellist. Then I thought of Carlos Vesper.

Carlos had disappeared from the action. Maybe because I just hadn't thought about him for a couple of days. I still didn't have any clear notion of why he lied to me about going out for a drink and being picked up on the Carmel Valley Road for speeding. He must have lied to me, the sonofabitch. Maybe he's in this thing up to his neck. Maybe he had discovered Della and was having an affair with her. In a moment of uncontrollable passion he bashed her with as ball peen hammer. Aw, that's a lot of crap.

Reiko had gone back into her domain and settled down to her computer. She was devoted to it. "You know why I use a Mac, Riordan? It's 'cause Apple is in Cupertino, that's why. Where my grandfather's property was. They bought it from him, you know. For a whole lot of money. That's why I've got money in the bank!" She emphasized those last three words.

Sitting at my desk, pretending to look through papers I had already looked through twenty or thirty times, I heard voices in the outer office. In a fraction of a second I identified them as Reiko's and, praise the Lord, Carlos Vesper's.

They came through my door, Reiko pushing the obviously reluctant Carlos ever so gently. He wouldn't look directly at me, but focussed more or less on the front edge of my desk.

"I . . . I've got a . . . sort of confession. You aren't gonna like it. And I've asked Reiko to protect me. She's a black belt, you know."

I stood up. I guess I bared my teeth.

"You know about that time I got caught speeding. I didn't want you to find out about that. But I didn't count on

Balestreri remembering who I was. He did. He called you. I had to tell you a story."

"Carlos, you were not headed for the Rio Grill to get a drink, were you? You were heading out Carmel Valley Road for some sort of nefarious business. Man, is there any reason why I should believe anything you tell me?"

He tried to look ashamed. It was hard for him. He had conned old people out of huge sums of money without remorse. Shame was a foreign emotion to Carlos Vesper.

"Riordan, I'm not used to having just one woman—even if she's a beautiful cellist with bow legs. So while Annie was rehearsing, and that was most of the time, I sorta looked around and somehow or other I found this gorgeous, susceptible young woman in Carmel Valley. I told her I was in investment advisor. She told me her daddy was one of the richest men in the Valley. What could I do?"

I sank slowly into my chair. "What has occasioned this confession, man? You're just not the *mea-culpa* type. Somebody has been putting the pressure on you. Who?"

His eyes shifted from the top of my desk to the ragged day-at-a-time calendar on the wall behind me, left over from 1986.

"Hey, you know it's not Tuesday, November twenty-seventh, don't you? Why. . . . ?"

"Give it to me straight, Carlos. Who's putting the pressure on you?"

He slumped into my hard and uncomfortable client's chair. He winced as his coccyx banged against the unyielding wood.

"You know the girl they found out at the Point? The one with her face smashed in. Cops have been chasing me around about that one. I didn't know that girl, Pat. Somebody told the Sheriff's guys that they saw me somewhere near. I wasn't. Truth is, I was with the woman from the Valley. They got me all wrong. But you understand, don't you? You know what kind of guy I am. You know I wouldn't really hurt anybody."

I stared at him. "Yeah, I know you. You'd cheerfully cheat an elderly widow out of her last few bucks. But I honestly doubt that you could bang a pretty woman in the face until it was bloody hamburger. I dunno, maybe you couldn't even hit one." I took a deep breath. "Okay, so what do you want me to do?"

"Just tell 'em. Just tell the cops what you know about me. They'll believe you. I swear Balestreri thinks you're some kind of saint."

"Does Anastasia know anything about this?"

"No, man."

"All right. I'll put in a word for you. But if what you've told me turns out to be bullshit, I'll beat the hell out of you with every blunt instrument I can get my hands on."

"That goes for me, too, " said Reiko.

30

"What are you going to do about the cockroach man, Riordan?"

BALESTRERI was on the phone. "You know, Pat, I kind of agree with you in spite of myself. Vesper is a consummate liar. We all know that. But a killer? Never in the world. It's just that somebody reported having seen him in the general vicinity of where the dead woman was found. It was an anonymous call. Coulda been the killer himself. You never know."

I had called him to report that Carlos had visited me with what I considered to be a valid alibi. "I'm just telling you what he told me, Tony. He is a strange beast, but, as you say, unlikely to kill anybody, let alone smash a pretty girl's face up. That's Carlos's one serious weakness. Pretty women."

I could hear another voice in the background and Balestreri mumbling something in reply. "Hey, Riordan, ever hear of a guy named Gregor Samsa?" he asked.

My God. The weirdo was back. The cockroach man who had come to me in the night and introduced himself as a character out of Kafka. "I'm afraid so, pal. Where'd you get that name?"

"The guy came in here. Said he'd been to the Carmel cops,

but they just politely showed him the door. Is the guy some sort of crazy?"

"He puts people off with the name. It's a character in a story by a Czech named Kafka. A character who turns into a cockroach."

"Shit!" said Balestreri. "He looked like a cockroach. Kept telling us he had the real skinny on the feud between Blum and Bialystock. Claims nobody believes him but there was a long-standing hate between the two because of some soprano. Both of 'em in love with her, he says. Real blood enemies, he says."

I had completely discounted Samsa's story by this time. But his perseverance with the police nudged me a little. Could it be possible that there was something in the tale of the unrequited passion that both men had for the same woman, who sailed away and left both of them sobbing on the dock?

"What did you do with him?" I asked.

"Thanked him very much and sent him home. Or wherever he's staying. He claimed to be a piano player."

"Did you get an address?"

"Let's see. Something here." Shuffling of paper. "Yeah, here it is. He's at an address on Lincoln Street in Carmel. One of those places the Bach people rent. He's probably in with a bunch of other musical types."

He gave me the house location and description, which is the only way you can find anybody in Carmel. As I no doubt have mentioned before, having no street addresses, no mail delivery and no streetlights creates a uniqueness that is some-times painful, but it has its advantages. If you want one of us, you have to go to some trouble to find us. Delivery people, FedEx and UPS all know the town by heart.

I have been involved in some pretty crazy murder cases. Nothing simple, ever. But that's usually why I'm involved. Some guy shoots some other guy in a bar fight, the cops pick the shooter up and book him, the court tries him, and most times he gets long hard jail time. But I always get things that involve lovers and other strangers.

Well, why not. Every life needs a little excitement. If I had not flunked the bar exam, I'd be a lawyer. Nobody loves lawyers. Or I could have been a politician. Ugh, what a thought!

Reiko came in and destroyed my daydream.

"What are you going to do about the cockroach man, Riordan? Don't you think there's something in his story?" She had been listening in, as usual. There seems to be nothing I can do about that. There isn't a call that comes through that she doesn't listen in to. She may be using the modem on our other line, but she suspends all action when the phone rings.

"What do you think we ought to do, Reiko-san? The guy's a pure psycho in my book. Delusional. Borderline. Paranoid. Whatever else you can think of. What can you think of?"

She perched on a corner of my desk. Somehow, when she does that with those short skirts and good legs, it makes me just a touch uncomfortable.

"Okay," she began, "what if the guy is a straight arrow, trying to give you information that really has a bearing on the case? And it sounds so far out that you just dismiss it. But maybe it's true. Whaddaya gonna do? I think you've got to pursue it further. Let's ask around and see if anybody has anything good or bad to say about Gregor Samsa."

So we decided to make the rounds.

We went first to the house on Ninth Avenue to see Bialystock.

"Come in, Mr. Riordan," said the first violinist. "How can I help you?"

"You know a man who calls himself Gregor Samsa?"

Bialystock smiled wanly. "Of course. He calls himself that because that is his name. Poor fellow. His parents burdened him with the name and he has been laughed at upon occasion during his entire life. He is an adequate accompanist. I have known him a long time."

"Would it surprise you to learn that he came to me with a disturbing story about your relationship with Theodore Blum? Would he have some reason to know that your professed amicable relationship with Blum was phony?"

"I would not be surprised by anything Samsa would say. He's a weak man, handicapped with short legs and small hands. Terrible for a pianist. He has remained in music by the skin of his teeth. I suppose it has affected his mind."

It seemed apparent that Bialystock was being cagey about the cockroach man. Nothing you could put your finger on, but a look of suspicion and anger in his eyes.

"Well, thank you, Mischa. Just checking. No special reason. Thank you again."

"Wait a minute," said Reiko. "Samsa told my partner that you and he were old friends. That he knew that you both were in love with the same woman. Was that true?"

Bialystock glared at her. "That is a private thing, young woman. Please let the past be the past. The three of us are mourning the loss of Della Fitzgerald. It was a terrible shock. She was an . . . adequate second violin. Please leave us to our sadness."

And he shut the door firmly. Didn't exactly slam it, you understand. Just shut it with emphasis.

We walked out to the car.

"Where to next, shamus?" asked Reiko.

"Let's talk to Anastasia."

We drove up out of the tiny canyon that was the north end of Ninth Street to Torres, right to Eighth Avenue, down the hill to Lincoln.

Once again we approached the small rental house occupied by my old buddy Carlos Vesper and his love, the beautiful cellist Anastasia Hawkins. The first light knock brought Anastasia to the door.

"Hello!" she said, with the rising inflection of surprise. "Carlos isn't here. I don't know where he is. I'm worried about him."

"We didn't come to see Carlos, honey. Just you. Have to ask you about a piano player named Gregor Samsa."

She looked amused.

"Isn't that awful? To saddle a child with a name like that. It's a good thing that most school kids have never heard of

Kafka. Think what a terrible time that man would have had. What about Samsa?"

"You know him?"

"Of course. I think all of us here at the Festival know each other. We've met in so many different places. It's like a sort of class reunion every time we meet. You know, at different events like this one. It's not always the same class, but you get to know everybody."

"Do you know if Samsa was a friend of Teddy Blum and Mischa Bialystock?"

"I'm sure that's true. They're . . . they were all about the same age, I guess."

We were still standing at the door. Reiko elbowed me aside to ask her own question: "Everybody we've talked to about the two of them has told us that that long feud was just a put-on. Something they cooked up between them. The only person who has told us—and incidentally, the police—that the feud was real and truly bloodthirsty . . . was Samsa. Why would he do that?"

Anastasia seemed stunned. "I don't know. You mean he said that Teddy would kill Mischa . . . or Mischa would kill Teddy?"

"Right on the nose, ma'am. That's the information we got from the cockroach man."

"All I can say is, Gregor has always been deeply resentful of other, more gifted musicians. But I can't believe he could be moved to violence. I'm sure he didn't kill Teddy Blum."

"That's not exactly what we were after, Annie," I put in. "What we're really looking for is somebody who could back up Samsa's story. That Blum and Bialystock really hated each other. And that possibly Mischa could be the criminal. We've got a murder and a suicide that might hook together. But the suicide was extremely weird. Blum's death appeared to be natural, but I'm not altogether sure about that. What we're after is hard cold facts about the reality of the relationships that existed among these people."

Anastasia sucked in her breath. "Do you mean that violinist who was killed so brutally? I've been reading about that in the paper."

"Yep. She was in Bialystock's quartet. You didn't know her?"

"No. She was one of the few people here that I had never met before."

Reiko pushed us both in and saw to it that we sat down. "It's drafty out there," she said. Then she addressed herself to Anastasia. "Everybody here has heard rumors or had anonymous telephone calls about somebody dying during an event at the Bach Festival, right?"

"Yes. Everybody I've talked to."

"But nobody has actually died yet, right?"

"So," my partner was pacing back and forth in front of us as we sat, "we really haven't had the big show yet, have we?"

31

What a character! Nobody like her.

B Y this time we were in the middle of the Bach Festival and it was hard to find a place in Carmel where one couldn't hear some instruments being tuned or the voice of a conductor shouting at a rehearsal. Not that this was a bad thing. It's part of the consummate charm of this village. When there's something going on, it's going on all over the place. When the Concours d'Elegance is in session there are gorgeous antique cars rolling through the town. When the AT&T Golf Tournament (I've still got a compulsion to call it The Crosby) is being played on the courses in the Del Monte Forest, you can run into John Travolta or Fran Tarkenton in the drug store. When the football season is over you can often find John Madden lounging on the bench outside Bruno's Market. You have to learn to take a lot of things for granted.

Carmel is one mile square, more or less, allowing for some zig-zags in the city line. In a way it's a small town, where you get to know everybody. It used to be a sort of artist colony, but there are galleries all over full of what my friend Armand Colbert refers to as non-art. "Patrick, my boy," he says, "there is no bad art or good art. There is simply art and non-art." I have never found out who buys the non-art, but somebody does. After all, there's still a market for "Dogs Playing Poker."

But I'm drifting again. As I said, the Festival was about half over. Crowds were coming and going, depending on what they had bought tickets for and where they were from. I was still waiting for something shocking to happen during the various concerts. Reiko and I were conscientiously attending everything but the lectures. I have to admit I learned a lot about some composers I'd never heard of. But I'll be quick to acknowledge that I drowsed through some events. It's hard to fall asleep during a Bach composition, though. Fugues keep changing. Pianissimo to fortissimo and like that. During one evening I longed for something by Aaron Copland.

I had just about made up my mind that it was all just a nasty gag cooked up by some disgruntled musician to keep everybody on edge. But they all seemed so tranquil and dedicated. Oh, there was excitement during the fast and furious passages of some of the compositions. But at no time did anything blow up. Nor did anybody drop dead.

"Look, partner, I'm getting pretty sick of all this stuff," said Reiko, after one afternoon concert featuring a piece that was so mournful and melancholy that she felt like slashing her wrists when it was over. "I don't think anything is going to happen. It's been just a big sick joke. Let's forget it."

"There's another week left, "I said," we've got to ride it out. If we don't, I'll have been remiss as far as Roger Carrington is concerned, and we've collected money from Carlos to protect his lady love. Although I'm not sure she is anymore."

"Is what?" Reiko asked.

"His lady love. I saw him just this morning having coffee at Wishart's Bakery with a blonde lady who was carrying a flute case."

"Forget Carlos! The bastard is a womanizer of the worst kind. I don't like the word 'womanizer.' It smacks too much of male domination. Bad word. I won't use it again." She tilted her head up and squared her shoulders.

What a character! I thought about Helen, my only wife, who died so many years ago. Reiko was a lot like her. That's what we look for, I guess, when we lose one we love, if indeed that love is honest. Somebody like the one lost.

As unenthusiastic as we were, we were still keeping tabs on Bialystock and his friends, Gregor Samsa, and, for good measure, Anastasia and Carlos. It grieved me to think of Annie as a possible suspect in this thing, but I had to keep her in the file.

The whole thing was getting to be a big bore. What had started out with so much promise showed every sign of fizzling out. Even during some of the music I liked, I found my thoughts drifting to other things.

I was walking alone from the Sunset Center theatre one night after a particularly soporific concert when I became aware of somebody close behind me. Nobody ever follows me. I follow people. That's my job sometimes. But I could hear the footsteps and even the sound of heavy breathing.

"Excuse me, please," said a voice behind me, familiar, but unrecognizable, "Mr. Riordan, may I have a word with you?"

I stopped and turned very slowly to look into the face of Feodor Chomsky, the cello player of Bialystock's quartet. I should say I looked up into the face of Chomsky, for the man was at least six-five. Funny I hadn't noticed that he was so tall when I saw him with the other members of his group.

"Here?" I asked. "Now? Kind of a strange place for a conversation."

We were standing at the corner of Eighth and San Carlos, by the Sunset Center parking lot. Groups of people were passing us chattering about the concert I had just dozed at.

"You have suggestions?" said Chomsky.

"Yeah. Let's go to my place. Up the hill."

Whether it was especially circumspect or not, I couldn't think of any other place where we could talk in quiet in Carmel at ten o'clock at night. Sure, the whole town closes down, except for a few bars. But I had a feeling that this conversation was going to be very interesting, indeed.

32

"Why are you telling me this?"

WE walked silently up Eighth Avenue, across Junipero, across Torres to Santa Fe and turned right to the dead end.

"You live here?" said Chomsky, incredulous. "We have been neighbors all this time and you do not tell us. You can look down on the house where we are staying and watch our every movement."

"Not really. I'm not home all the time. I do have an office in Monterey. But I have to confess I've watched you and your friends come and go from time to time."

I led him into my living room and pointed to the couch. "Please sit."

There is a lamp on in the corner that I never turn off. No special reason that I can think of. Maybe it's so I can tell right away if there's a power failure. We have 'em now and then at the most unexpected times. I keep flashlights on strategic tables, anticipating a blackout.

I settled in my favorite chair. "Now, then, Mr. Chomsky, what's on your mind."

For whatever reason I didn't feel uncomfortable with this

man. He was big, that's true. But his voice was soft and un-
threatening.

"I have been very disturbed," he began, "about the death
of Della. She was so young, so talented. I was twice her age,
but I think I was in love with her. I didn't tell her. I made no
moves on her. I was an old man to her. An old man whom she
could not imagine as a lover. But . . . "

He stretched his long legs out and locked his hands behind
his head.

"Go on, please. What did you do?"

"Nothing. But Mischa knew how I felt. He talked to me
about my feelings. He sympathized. I think Mischa was
attracted to her himself. I know he was jealous of her."

"Jealous? Why?"

"As you know, Mischa has a progressive disease—
Parkinson's—that has interfered with his music. Sooner or
later it will disable him altogether. A violinist with a violent
tremor in his left hand is lost. Della was so gifted. She was a
talent, Mr. Riordan. I have no doubt that she would have
emerged as a soloist of the highest quality in time."

Chomsky's face was in shadow and I couldn't really see his
expression. "Why are you telling me this?" I asked.

"I don't know, " he answered. His voice had changed. His
English which had been unaccented, began to show signs of his
Russian origin. "It is a tragedy to lose one so young and so
gifted. But it is even greater tragedy to imagine that that person's life was taken by a friend."

"That's what you think? Mischa killed Della?"

"Mischa, maybe. Or Maria. Or that insane accompanist
Samsa."

"Samsa you consider a friend, then?"

Feodor Chomsky smiled ruefully. "Not really. But I have
known him for a long time, and I know that despite the mild
facade he displays he is capable of wicked, wicked deeds. I
know of at least one promising singer he destroyed by striking
wrong notes as he accompanied her and insisting that it was
she, not he, who was off key. The poor woman—who would

really have been nothing but a second rate contralto—was driven to the edge of madness, lost her voice completely, and now sells real estate in Orange County. Riordan! You look skeptical. You do not believe me."

I closed my eyes and pulled at my right ear. "Feodor, you are either a consummate liar, or the story you have just told is completely bizarre. Which?"

"I do embroidery on some of my better tales of the music world. And that was some of my best needlework. Good story, though, don't you think?"

"But why? You said you had some firm suspicions of several people, including Samsa. Give it to me straight, my friend, or I'll show you a short cut to your accommodations off my back deck."

A look of dark Russian melancholy crossed the man's face. "Samsa is a suspect because he, too, was in love with Della Fitzgerald. He came to our rehearsals. Not those in the house, but the formal rehearsals in one of the rooms at the Sunset Center. He stood in the back of the room, or if there was a chair, he would sit down. He followed Della like a schoolboy. He was—and is—an enigma."

I pressed: "But what about Blum? And Schmidt? Did he have some sort of grudge against them?"

He was genuinely surprised. "What do you mean. I was informed that Blum's death was from natural causes and that Schmidt committed suicide."

"Maybe," I said. "I'm not convinced. It's hard for me to get it into my head that two guys who were so disliked by so many could conveniently expire so dramatically during a special occasion in which each was involved."

"You are a fool, I think, Mr. Riordan," said the Russian cellist as he unfolded his long frame from the couch. "Tell me, is there another way to get to the house down below? A short cut?"

I explained that he could follow the path through the small grove of city-owned trees at the dead end of the street. I even lent him a flashlight.

"You can toss it on my lower deck in the morning," I said, cheerfully.

Chomsky said not another word, and left my house.

33
"Look at Mischa!"

THINGS were gettin' pretty dull. I was bored. We were very near to the end of the Bach Festival and, aside from the discovery of three corpses, nothing had happened. Well, I really don't mean that. You cannot say nothing happened when people die in strange ways.

But the main event, the thing that everybody had been expecting, the death during a concert—just hadn't materialized. It was all a big hoax, I thought. But why in God's name would somebody create a hoax that involved three dead bodies, one of which was obviously murdered.

The schedule was drawing to a close. The biggest thing left was the big concert on the last Saturday evening of the Festival. Nearly all the musicians were to be brought together to perform highlights of the great affair. Reiko and I decided to take in this one together.

The usual mobs were milling around in the parking lot at the Sunset Center, some of the people actually in semi-formal clothes, black tie and cocktail dresses. The evening was warm, and while some of the tuxedo clad males were squirming in their tight collars, the ladies were perfectly comfortable in low-cut numbers with spaghetti straps.

At last somebody got the signal and the crowd moved slowly into the theatre. The hum of conversation was at a high level. Finally, the auditorium was filled and the crowd settled down and became silent.

The orchestra filed onto the stage briskly. I noticed right away that it was bigger than usual and there was scarcely room for all the instruments. Immediately I looked for members of my favorite string quartet, and, sure enough, spotted Mischa, Maria, and Feodor in separate sections. Everybody was getting into the act.

The conductor strode out and took his place on the podium. He faced the audience for the prescribed smile and enthusiastic reception. Then he turned and raised his baton. He paused, looking right and left. Then he brought the baton down and the orchestra began to play.

I don't know what the composition was, but it was loud. I don't think it was Bach, but who am I to say. It wasn't a fugue, anyhow.

Fugues make me very nervous.

The concert went through a number of excerpts from other pieces that had been featured during the Festival. I recognized a few. Mostly, I watched members of the Bialystock Quartet. If something were going to happen, I had the feeling that it was going to happen here and pretty soon.

Reiko sat beside me, mouth slightly open, small hand beating time on her lap. While I was looking at her, her eyes grew wide and her body stiffened.

"Look!" she said, in a hoarse whisper. "Look at Mischa!"

Bialystock had risen from his chair, still playing. Other musicians in his section were looking at him, distracted. The conductor was glaring at him.

Mischa pushed the chair to his left with such a violent force that it caused the violinist sitting next to him to drop his bow and catch himself as he slid to the floor. Bialystock, like a man in a trance moved out on the apron of the stage, still playing, although many of the others had stopped and the conductor had lowered his baton in dismay.

When he reached the edge of the stage, he stopped playing abruptly. He looked out into the audience wildly. His legs seemed to lose all their strength and he collapsed, face down, still holding bow and instrument, which dangled off the stage.

The members of the audience were on their feet instantly. Musicians rushed to the aid of their fallen colleague. A roar of sound came up in the auditorium.

Chomsky and Maria rushed from their places in the orchestra to their friend and bent over his body. They dragged him onto the stage so that his bow and his instrument fell from his hands to the floor of the auditorium. One music lover leaped forward to catch the Stradivarius, but missed it by a fraction of an inch. The precious instrument hit the floor and the sound of splintering wood was sickening.

It had all taken place in less than a minute, and finally I was galvanized into action. I could get my legs and arms to move, so I dashed for the stage.

"Is he dead?" I asked Chomsky.

"No. Not yet. Dying, perhaps, but not yet dead." The cellist looked genuinely distraught. Maria had covered her face and was sobbing violently.

"Somebody call 911," I yelled. Somebody already had, I guess, because I could hear the ambulance siren faintly over the noise of the crowd. Soon the paramedics came rushing down the main aisle and clustered around Bialystock's body.

"Still breathing," I heard one of them say. "Pulse is slow, but fairly strong. I think he can make it to the hospital. Charlie, start an IV."

I still can't remember how much time had elapsed since Mischa wandered out of the violin section and hit the deck. But everything happened so damn fast! Reiko was tugging at my sleeve.

"Let's get outa here, Pat. Up to Community Hospital, I think."

She grabbed my hand and dragged me to the car.

34

"He cannot be saved."

I DON'T know how we did it, but I think Reiko just pushed people out of the way as we found our way through the milling throng to my rusty Mercedes two-seater.

"Hurry, unlock it, Riordan," she urged.

"It isn't locked. I never lock it. What's to steal?"

With a look of pure disgust, she opened the driver's side door and shoved me in. Before I could find the ignition key, she was beside me.

"Get a move on!"

"There's no reason to hurry. They're taking the guy to the emergency room. They won't let anybody in there who isn't family."

"We'll tell 'em we're family."

"I won't do that, kid. I simply won't do that. I don't look anything like a relative of Mischa Bialystock and you, for God's sake, family?"

"Adopted. Viet Nam war orphan. You people can't tell one Asian from another, anyhow."

I shut up. No point trying to argue with Reiko. I drove as

fast as I dared to Community Hospital. She kept stabbing the floorboards with her accelerator foot impatiently.

"Get a move on, Riordan. You're wimping!"

I ignored her. We got to the hospital at a respectable speed. We arrived just as the gurney from the ambulance was disappearing into the swinging doors of the emergency room.

I tried to find a parking place in the enormous hospital lot. My luck was working. A car pulled out fairly up the hill, near the hospital. Reiko was out almost before the Mercedes stopped rolling.

"C'mon," she yelled. "You can at least jog. It won't kill you."

She was twenty yards ahead of me by this time, and out of sight in three seconds.

When I reached the emergency room, Reiko had already alienated the reception nurse who had told her several times that she couldn't get in to see Mr. Bialystock, but she could wait and be informed. About that time Maria and Feodor arrived. Maria was immediately led into the room where Mischa lay. Feodor, however, was asked to stay in the waiting room.

While Reiko steamed and paced, I went to Feodor Chomsky. "What happened?" I asked.

He had a far-away look in his heavy-lidded eyes as he turned to respond to my question.

"I . . . I'm not sure. I think I know, but I'm not sure."

"Did Mischa have a heart problem?"

"No. No heart trouble."

"What do you think? Stroke, maybe?"

Chomsky stretched his considerable length out in the small waiting-room chair. His head was against the painted wall, his eyes closed tightly.

"You might have been told that the critic Schmidt had a malignant brain tumor. I saw an article in the local newspaper which attributed his suicide to that malady."

"Yes, " I said. "Woman I know at the *Herald* told me just that."

"It was pure rot, Mr. Riordan. Just another of Schmidt's tales. He was a truly evil man. Actually, it is poor Mischa who has the tumor. As well as Parkinson's disease."

"Why . . . ?"

"Why would Schmidt do such a thing? To gain the sympathy of a writer, perhaps. He knew that Mischa was very ill. He just chose to borrow one of Mischa's ailments to gain a little sympathy."

I looked up at Reiko who was furiously arguing with the receiving nurse again. The nurse was on the verge of calling security to throw my partner out bodily. Chomsky had lapsed into silence again, so I left him and went to Reiko.

"Slow down, Reiko-san. You're not gettin' yourself anywhere but thrown out. This is not the time and place to toss your weight around. What weight you've got, that is. Think about it. It's the end of a shift here. These people have been fielding distraught friends and relatives for hours. Come on. Sit down."

She did so, reluctantly.

We waited for a couple of hours. The magazines were all at least a couple of months old. I had read the newspaper. I guess the only reason I was not bored is that I was mulling over the fact that Evan Schmidt had lied about his illness. Why? And why should he borrow a malignant tumor from Mischa Bialystock? The guy was very strange.

At last, a nurse came out and motioned Chomsky to come with her into the treatment area. Reiko jumped up immediately and ran to the nurse's desk. The shift had changed by this time.

"Hey, they let him in. To see Mr. Bialystock. He's no relative. How come?"

The nurse was calm and pleasant. "Mrs. Bialystock asked that he be allowed in."

That stumped Reiko, I guess. She couldn't think of anything to say, so she sat down beside me and pouted.

Another hour passed. Or was it two hours? I squinted to look at my watch because I didn't have my little reading glasses. What was it? Three A.M.? Four A.M.?

My God, were we going to see dawn break over Monterey?

The door opposite us opened slowly and Maria Genovese Bialystock appeared. She came directly to us.

"Mischa is dying," she said, almost inaudibly. "He cannot be saved. He took something. Some sort of poison. Something that would destroy him faster than the terrible sicknesses he had. He wouldn't tell me what." She managed a wan smile. "Afraid I might do the same thing, I guess. Mischa can barely speak. But he wants to talk to you. Remember, this is a dying man."

She led us through the door into the treatment area with a nod from the receiving nurse. We walked past several stalls where patients were being attended to. Maria steered us into the last stall on the right.

Mischa Bialystock looked like a dead man already. His eyes were sunken, his complexion was dead white. He was barely breathing.

"It is Riordan and Miss Masuda, Mischa," said Maria.

The dying man opened his eyes. He opened them wide. I didn't think a man in this condition could have such life in his eyes. They were luminous.

"I am very weak, but I think I have strength enough to tell you what I must tell you," he said.

We listened as he spoke, not daring to interrupt.

"The virulent hate between Teddy Blum and me was genuine. I believe that my old friend Samsa told you that, didn't he? He shouldn't have, but he did, yes? No matter.

"I knew that Teddy had the pacemaker installed in Istanbul. He had been told that he must care for it, or it would fail. I suspect it wasn't very good in the first place, but Teddy was negligent. He never had the device checked. I thought it must be losing its power. Then I read somewhere that cellular telephones may be dangerous to wearers of pacemakers.

"I went to Teddy's hotel room. When I arrived, he had just phoned you, Mr. Riordan. I pretended to be on a mission of peace. And I was carrying a cellular telephone.

"I also had a bottle of very good brandy. Teddy was always

a poor drinker. I knew if he had two or three drinks he would get drowsy, easily fall asleep. That is what happened. While he was asleep, I placed the cellular telephone on his left breast, drew out the antenna, and turned on the power. I called Maria. Of course, I did not tell her where I was or what I was doing. We talked for perhaps ten minutes. It was apparently enough for a very weak pacemaker. When I finished my call, Teddy was dead. Whether it was my action that killed him or just the failure of his device, I don't know. But I knew I meant to kill him.

"Schmidt was another matter. He was healthy, strong as an ox. I had to lay my plans carefully. I went to his hotel room with a slender knife. I had taken care to wear a pair of light gloves. I accused Schmidt of helping to destroy my career by mocking my incurable disease. The man laughed. He had no respect for me. I knew that. He couldn't have realized that he had anything to fear. He was laughing when I drove the blade into his belly and ripped it up. He did not live two minutes.

"I stripped the gross body naked and carried away the bloody clothing in a hotel laundry bag. I carefully wiped the knife and placed it in his right hand so that his fingerprints would be on it. Then I tossed the knife under the bed, but positioned so that it could actually have fallen out of his hand as he died. I stripped off the gloves and put them in the laundry bag with Schmidt's clothes. I carried the bag out of the hotel and placed it in the first trash can I came to."

Bialystock was growing weaker by the second. His voice was fading and he coughed frequently. But he was making a heroic effort. He had another tale to tell.

With great effort, he began: "The thing I am truly guilty of . . . is the vicious murder of Della Fitzgerald." His voice, which was fast disappearing, broke, and he coughed.

"I was in love . . . with Della. Foolish, foolish. Maria . . . knew. I was also jealous of Della's . . . enormous talent. She . . . would become a concert soloist, I knew. I . . . could barely control my fingers as I played. Della should have been playing my parts."

The strain was almost too much. Mischa gasped between sentences, often between words.

But he went on: "I tried . . . to show Della my love. I touched her. She was . . . shocked. She pushed me away. Then I . . . went mad. I hit her. I kept hitting her . . . I . . ."

"Mischa, stop!" said Maria. "You don't have to do this."

He heard his wife's voice, but did not respond. His face contorted as if he were crying, but no tears came. He made a terrible, chilling sound. And he died.

35

She's moving in! Hooray! Hooray!

IT was about a week later. Reiko and I were sitting in the office doing nothing. We had nothing to do.

Carlos, true to his word, had paid us the additional "thou." The Festival was over, and the sound of music was not now pervasive in the Carmel atmosphere. The distinguished visitors, musicians and music lovers alike, had all left town. They would probably all be back in another year.

Funny, the local merchants are not at all enthusiastic about the Bach Festival visitors. "They're all tire kickers," said a restaurateur of my acquaintance. "They order from prices on the menu. A lot of 'em come to the early dinners, the excuse being that they've got to get to a concert."

The keeper of a high fashion shop told me: "They do not buy. They look. I like better the people who come for the Laguna Seca races. Perhaps the motorcycle people are the best." And on and on. There was general agreement that the best money people are the ones who come for the Concours d'Elegance. They have to be loaded to afford those great cars.

"Dull, ain't it," said Reiko.

"It'll pick up," I said, not at all sure. "It's August. It's always dull in August."

She came over and sat on my desk in the manner that disturbs me so much.

"What happened?" I knew she was asking about the Bialystock affair.

"Man just went berserk. Incurably ill. Lost everything. Decided to get rid of all the things that ailed him that he could get rid of. Knew he was going to die anyhow."

"But why the girl? Why Della?"

"Like I said. He was crazy at the end. He lost it. Happens."

She shook her head. "I don't care. He really didn't have a reason to kill a beautiful and talented woman like that. Crazy or not."

"He didn't have to tell us about it, either."

Long ago, in my Santa Clara days, I had considered the priesthood. What? Did I look like a priest to Bialystock? Was it like confession? But Mischa was Jewish. You never know. Like Greg's friend, the Baptist rabbi.

We closed up shop early. No use sitting and staring at each other, asking questions that didn't have answers.

I took Reiko to dinner at Montrio, the newest occupant of the old Monterey fire house on Calle Principal. First time I'd had the nerve to spend that kind of money for weeks.

She decided to go home that evening. I tried, rather mildly to talk her out of it, but didn't succeed. Well enough. I wasn't feeling particularly hormonal anyhow. I got a quick kiss at the door, but couldn't resist asking her again: "Why don't you just move to my place, kid. I'm lonely. I need company."

"Not yet. Maybe some day. G'night."

Next morning I was awakened by a very loud sound, something between my doorbell and somebody beating a garbage can lid with a hammer. Anyhow, it sounded like that when it woke me up.

I dragged myself to the door in my nightshirt. I got this great deal on these cotton nightshirts from this mail order place in Florida. I've got a dozen of 'em. All blue.

Reiko was waiting when I opened the door. Just standing

there with a smirk, waiting. Obviously with something in mind. Something particularly Reikoish.

"So come in. I'll fix some coffee. What time is it?"

"Just after nine. You sleep too much. But you're pretty old, aren't you?" She had that look of devilment that she often got when she was putting one over on me.

She came in and went straight to my dining room table. "Okay, where's the coffee?"

"I have to make it, dammit." Which I did.

She took a sip, made a face. "Tea's much better."

"Why didn't you ask for tea? You're pushin' me, kid."

She looked coy. "You asked me again to move in with you last night."

"Yes, I asked you to move in. I keep asking you. I'm very lonely. I don't like being lonely. Goddammit, don't you know that."

I heard a noise at the door. Some kind of noise I couldn't identify.

"Well . . . I just thought I'd do something about that."

My heart leapt up as I thought I beheld a rainbow in my life. She's moving in! Hooray, hooray!

She had this sneaky smile on her face as she rose from the table and walked to the front door.

Reiko paused for a moment and stood with a hand on the knob. "I don't want you to be lonely. So I brought you a friend."

She opened the door to admit the absolutely frowziest, mud-colored canine I had ever seen.

"My God!" I said. "A dog. I got a whole house with wall-to-wall carpet. How'm I gonna housebreak a dog?"

"Princess is a lady. She is already housebroken. She loves people. She'll probably even love you."

The shaggy animal came to me and put her nose up my nightshirt.

"This is a substitute for you?"

"Not really, Riordan. Temporarily."

"Where'd she come from?"

"Friend of mine had to move to San Francisco for a new job. Couldn't take Princess. You're just lucky."

With that, she kissed me quickly and was gone. Princess was wagging her tail.

"See you at the office, shamus." Reiko waved cheerily.

The shaggy dog leaned against my leg as I closed the door.

"Hello, Princess. Glad to see you. I think." I reached down to pat her on the head.

She smiled and wagged her tail again, briskly.

I'll get you for this, Reiko, I thought. Yeah, maybe I'll get you here, with your Japanese garden and your shaggy friend. And, by God, I did. But that's another story.

Roy Gilligan lives in Carmel-by-the-Sea, California, but steadfastly refuses to say Carmel-by-the-Sea out loud. He has a totally useless degree in Early European History from the University of Cincinnati and a mess of credits from NYU, Eastern Kentucky, Indiana University, San Jose State, and the University of California at Santa Cruz. He was a radio announcer when they were actually called "radio announcers." He also appeared on TV as actor and newscaster. He has written a lot of stuff for various publications. He's still living with his first wife, Jane, and dotes on his two grandchildren. He won't lie about his age if you ask him.

ORDER INFORMATION:

This or any other title from Brendan Books can be ordered direct from the publisher. Just name the book and send $8.95 plus $1.50 postage and handling to:

Brendan Books
P.O. Box 221143
Carmel, California 93922

If you're curious, consult the page opposite this book's title for the list.